PAYBACK

PAYBACK

FROM THE AUTHORS OF TRAITOR

ANDY McNAB
and ROBERT RIGBY

G. P. PUTNAM'S SONS

G. P. PUTNAM'S SONS
A division of Penguin Young Readers Group.
Published by The Penguin Group.
Penguin Group (USA) Inc., 375 Hudson Street, New York, NY 10014, U.S.A.
Penguin Group (Canada), 90 Eglinton Avenue East, Suite 700, Toronto, Ontario, Canada M4P 2Y3
(a division of Pearson Penguin Canada Inc.). Penguin Books Ltd, 80 Strand, London WC2R 0RL,
England. Penguin Ireland, 25 St. Stephen's Green, Dublin 2, Ireland (a division of Penguin Books
Ltd.). Penguin Group (Australia), 250 Camberwell Road, Camberwell, Victoria 3124, Australia
(a division of Pearson Australia Group Pty Ltd). Penguin Books India Pvt Ltd, 11 Community
Center, Panchsheel Park, New Delhi - 110 017, India. Penguin Group (NZ), Cnr Airborne and
Rosedale Roads, Albany, Auckland 1310, New Zealand (a division of Pearson New Zealand Ltd).
Penguin Books (South Africa) (Pty) Ltd, 24 Sturdee Avenue, Rosebank, Johannesburg 2196,
South Africa. Penguin Books Ltd, Registered Offices: 80 Strand, London WC2R 0RL, England.

Library of Congress Cataloging-in-Publication Data
McNab, Andy. Traitor: payback / by Andy McNab and Robert Rigby.   p. cm.
Summary: As teenage suicide bombers terrorize England, seventeen-year-old Danny tries to
help his grandfather, an ex-SAS explosives expert falsely accused of being a traitorous spy by
the government's intelligence agencies.
[1. Spies—Fiction. 2. Espionage—Fiction. 3. Terrorism—Fiction. 4. Grandfathers—Fiction.
5. Orphans—Fiction. 6. Great Britain. Army. Special Air Service—Fiction. 7. England—
Fiction.] I. Rigby, Robert. II. Title.
PZ7.M478792866Trh 2006   [Fic]—dc22   2005032657

ISBN 0-399-24465-4
1 3 5 7 9 10 8 6 4 2
First Impression

GLOSSARY

Bivvy bag	Gore-Tex sleeping cover
Bomb burst	Split up
Contact	In a firefight with the enemy
CTR	Close target recce
Dead ground	Ground that cannot be seen
Det	Detonator
DPM	Disruptive patter material
ERV	Emergency rendezvous
FARC	Colombian drug traffickers
FOB	Forward operating base
GSW	Gunshot wound
HE	High explosives
IBs	The elite of the Secret Intelligence Service
IED	Improvised explosive device
Int	Intelligence
LS	Landing strip
LUP	Lay-up point
Mag	A weapons magazine that holds the rounds
Make ready a weapon	To put a round in the chamber, ready to be fired
MCC	Marylebone Cricket Club
MI6	Secret Intelligence Service
MoD	Ministry of Defense
MP	Member of Parliament
MP5	Heckler and Koch 9 mm submachine gun
MPV	Multipurpose vehicle
NVGs	Night viewing goggles
OP	Observation post
PAD	Protection area defense
Pinged	When someone is first seen
RAF	Royal Air Force
Recce	Reconnaissance

The Regiment	What SAS soldiers call the SAS
Rounds	Bullets
RV	Rendezvous (meeting place)
Sit rep	Situation report
SOP	Standard operating procedure
On stag	On guard
Stand to	Get ready to be attacked
Tab	Forced march or speed march

SURVEILLANCE TALK

Complete	Inside any location—a car, building, etc.
Foxtrot	Walking
Held	Stopped but intending to move on—i.e. at traffic lights
Mobile	Driving
Net	The radio frequency the team talk on
Roger	OK or understood
Stand by! Stand by!	Informs the team something is happening
Static	Stopped
The trigger	Informs the team that the target is on the move

HACKING TALK

Exploits	Hackers' targets
Root access	When the hacker has control of the system under attack
Script kiddie	Novice hacker
Script	A program written by a hacker
Spoofing	Hiding a computer's IP address

FERGUS WATTS

AGE: 53

HEIGHT: Five feet eleven inches

PHYSICAL DESCRIPTION: Hair—gray; eyes—blue; build—lean, wiry; distinguishing physical marks—noticeable limp due to bullet wound in right thigh

BACKGROUND: Infantry. SAS, Warrant Officer, special skills—explosives. Tours of duty include—Northern Ireland (decorated), first Gulf conflict (decorated), Colombia. Recruited as a Deniable Operator ("K") to infiltrate FARC, Colombia. Cover story—traitor, "gone over" to rebels for money.

Watts's cover was deliberately blown by our PRIMARY TARGET. Watts wounded and captured after gun battle with Colombian antinarcotics police. Imprisoned by Colombian authorities. Subsequently led mass jailbreak. Returned to Britain, route and date unknown. Traced through grandson, Danny (see below). Captured but escaped from safe house with help from grandson and Elena Omolodon. Note: Information on Omolodon's involvement unknown to Secret Intelligence Service. Two operators and one civilian (Eddie Moyes, freelance reporter) killed during escape. Watts on run for past six months.

DANNY WATTS

AGE: 17

HEIGHT: Five feet ten inches

PHYSICAL DESCRIPTION: Hair—brown; eyes—blue; build—slim; distinguishing physical marks—none known

BACKGROUND: Orphaned at six, parents died in car crash. Various foster families until moved to Foxcroft, south London, residential home for teenagers, where he met Elena Omolodon. Applied for army officer training bursary. Rejected after interview with PRIMARY TARGET. Had never met grandfather but fed "traitor" story and located (method unknown). Assisted in escape of Fergus Watts. On run for past six months. Note: Elena Omolodon still resident at Foxcroft.

INTERIM OBJECTIVE: Still need to confirm who, if anyone outside THE FIRM, knew Fergus Watts was working as a K. Watts also remains potentially useful in operation to expose PRIMARY TARGET.

1

Big Ben struck midday as he walked through Parliament Square. The spring sun was warm, almost hot, but he kept his brand-new puffa jacket zipped up to the neck. A police car siren sounded, and he turned to watch the driver skillfully maneuver his vehicle through the snarl of traffic and on toward Westminster Bridge.

He was feeling slightly apprehensive, but at the same time elated. At last he was about to do something meaningful, something significant. Waiting at the pedestrian crossing, he smiled and gently squeezed the few twists of green garden twine nestling in the palm of his right hand. For comfort.

As the traffic lights turned to red and the green man flashed on, he crossed with the rest of the crowd waiting at the curbside. Japanese tourists walked with their camcorders at arm's length, watching their screens while filming the imposing, magnificent buildings. Motorbike couriers revved their engines, impatient for the lights to change.

He joined the line outside St. Stephen's Gate, the public access point to the Houses of Parliament. Armed police watched impassively as the line of visitors slowly shuffled toward the wide entrance doors leading to the X-ray machine and the metal detector blocking the corridor about fifteen meters inside the building.

Ahead of him was a small group of young women, some with babies in carriers strapped to their fronts, brandishing leaflets warning of the health hazards created by a newly opened landfill site and chatting animatedly about the imminent meeting with their local MP.

The line was in the sun, and tiny beads of perspiration dotted his upper lip, but still he kept his chunky Gap jacket zipped up. He looked smart: his hair was neatly combed, his trousers were immaculately pressed and his black shoes still shone with newness.

A thin trickle of sweat ran down the side of his head as he turned and smiled politely at a group of old-timers who were beginning to line up behind him. The women wore their best dresses and light coats and the men were in blazers, their old regimental insignias sewn onto the breast pocket and their highly polished medals hanging proudly above.

"You here for the tour too?" asked one of the men, fishing out a letter of invitation from his blazer pocket and unfolding it to reveal the embossed letterhead reading: HOUSE OF COMMONS.

"No," he answered softly.

"How old are you, son?" said the man.

"Seventeen."

The man nodded his admiration. "Well, it's good to see a youngster with an interest in politics," he said. "Makes a nice change these days."

"Oh, yes," he replied, his fingers caressing the twine in his hand. "I'm very interested in politics."

He turned back as the line moved closer to the large doors opening onto the grand corridor, where statues of statesmen through the ages lined both sides. Reporters and visitors were showing their credentials for entering the public areas before placing briefcases and bags on the X-ray machine and then stepping through the detector.

The group of young women was stopped by a white-shirted security guard and asked about the purpose of their visit. They named their MP and showed their letter of invitation and were allowed to move into the corridor toward the security checks.

The new shoes were pinching slightly, chafing his heels, but nothing could stop his joy as he stepped over the ancient threshold of Parliament, where a security guard was waiting to question him. "And what business do you have here today, sir?"

He smiled at the security guard and whispered a single word: "Martyrdom."

The guard leaned closer. "Sorry, sir, what name was that?"

He didn't reply, but pulled sharply at the twine that ran up his arm. St. Stephen's Gate erupted in a hail of flying glass, shattered statues and broken bodies.

2

BLOODY CARNAGE

The two-word headline was plastered across a photograph filling the entire front and back pages of the *Sun*.

The graphic picture showed a bewildered and blood-soaked woman survivor being helped away from the dust and debris of the shattered St. Stephen's Gate by an ashen-faced government minister. They were stepping over the twisted body of one of the victims. The minister's eyes bulged in disbelief; his jacket hung in shreds; one end of the bloodied bandage wrapped around his head dangled down to his shoulder.

Eight further pages were devoted solely to what the newspaper was calling "the Parliament Bomb Outrage."

There were photos of fallen masonry, shattered glass, buckled ironwork, the decapitated head of a stone statue, a single shiny black shoe. Heavily armed police officers were pictured manning hastily erected barriers, paramedics rushed toward ambulances with laden stretchers, an exhausted firefighter leaned against a wall with tears streaming down his face, white-suited scene-of-crime officers searched for forensic evidence amid the chaos and confusion.

There were photos of survivors and photos of the dead. Bodies lying in the dust. Rows of zipped-up body bags.

In the immediate aftermath of the bombing, television and radio news bulletins had suggested the death toll could reach between a hundred and fifty and two hundred, but in the hours that followed, the number of confirmed dead was put at sixty-four. More were still listed as missing and many more were fighting for their lives in hospital.

The suicide bomber had been quickly identified: his student railcard was found five meters from the spot where the bomb had exploded. But the discovery of the railcard, far from explaining the outrage, just added to the mystery. For Zeenan Khan had been no international terrorist or "sleeper" smuggled in from a terrorist hotbed like Afghanistan or the Middle East to await the order to strike from his masters.

Zeenan had been a seventeen-year-old A-level student from north London, and although he was of Pakistani origin and a Muslim, he had been born and bred in England. He *was* English. An Arsenal football scarf hung over his bed and on the bedroom walls were posters torn from *Loaded* magazine.

His devastated family were said to be too distressed to speak to the press and had gone into hiding, but they were described by neighbors as being "not political" and "proud to be British."

There were photos of Zeenan in his school uniform. His headmaster was quoted as being "shocked and struggling to believe that the bomber could really have been the level-headed student who had aced eight of his GCSEs and had been working hard for his A levels."

Somehow all the newspapers had managed to find a family portrait: Mum, dad, three kids—Zeenan the eldest—all smiling, happy, proud.

He was "just a normal boy," said a neighbor who refused to be named. "A quiet lad," said another. "Kept himself to himself, but very polite and never in any trouble."

Politicians, community and religious leaders were quoted. Everyone appealed for calm.

But for all the background information, comments and quotes, two vital questions remained unanswered: how had a seventeen-year-old Muslim schoolboy made, or obtained, an explosive device reckoned to be identical to those used by extremists in places like Jerusalem and Baghdad? And why had Zeenan Khan, a boy with everything to live for, chosen to step willingly into oblivion?

News of the bombing was dominating newspaper headlines and television news reports around the world. At a roadside bar between Badajoz and Huelva in southern Spain, two builders, Londoners in their twenties, were drinking tea and reading a copy of the *Sun* printed in Madrid that morning.

"It's unbelievable," said Paul as he scanned the pages. "It says here he had at least seven kilos of explosives strapped to him. What's the world coming to when kids no older than young Dean there are blowing themselves to pieces?"

"But they're not like Dean, are they?" boomed his mate Benny, who sounded as though he should be an East End street vendor. "They're different, these Muslims. It's a different mentality, a different attitude to life and death. We'll never understand it."

The two builders were customers at a tea bar by the side of the sun-baked road. It was not quite like the mobile cafés and burger bars seen at roadsides back in Britain. This was a more casual setup. A canvas awning sheltered a couple of trestle tables from the blistering Spanish sun. On the tables were propane gas-powered griddles, hot plates and an urn. Two Union flags drooped limply from extensions to the poles holding up the awning.

Paul and Benny, and anyone else who asked, knew the owner by the name of Frankie, a fifty-something Englishman. Frankie was helped out at the tea bar by his young nephew Dean, who was on his gap year before university.

That was the story. It was far from the truth.

Every evening, when business was over, Frankie and Dean would load the mobile tea bar into the back of their secondhand Toyota pickup truck and carry out routine antisurveillance drills as they drove back to their small rented house in the town of Valverde del Camino. The route back to the house was quiet and little used, but Frankie stuck to all speed limits and regularly checked his mirrors, taking a mental note of vehicles following for any length of time. A few miles before the town he would pull over to the side of the road so that any following vehicles were committed to passing. Once they got back to town, they would make a further check to see if any such vehicle was still being driven around or parked up anywhere near the house.

Accommodation had been easy to find: they had cash, the landlord wanted tenants and he wasn't bothered about inconveniences like references. Only when they had returned to the security of the white-walled house could Frankie and Dean revert to their true identities—Fergus Watts and his grandson Danny.

It was six months since they had last seen England, a long six months, especially for Danny. Six months in which answering to his assumed name had become second nature; six months in which the constant fear of ambush or attack had gradually subsided; six months in which he had got used to living an anonymous life; six months in which he had dreamed of returning home every single day.

But that was impossible—for now, at least.

For now, they had to wait. And watch. And take the same precautions Fergus had learned during his years in the SAS. For now, they would live a lie as Frankie and Dean. They would cook and make endless mugs of tea and coffee while listening to other people's conversations. About football. About the weather. About terrorist attacks in the heart of London.

"The thing is, Paul, the world's changed since 9/11," said Benny, continuing the heated discussion with his friend. "Terrorism has taken on a new dimension. Look at those other suicide bombers—you know, those Chechen Black Widows: they're not just prepared to die for their cause, they *want* to die for it. It's a holy thing for them—it's a . . . a . . ." He was floundering for the right word.

"A jihad," said Frankie, looking up from the hot plate.

"That's it, that's the word," said Benny. "Jihad." He looked at Frankie. "What d'you reckon about all this then, Frankie?"

"Don't ask me," said Frankie, going back to his hot plate. "I just cook."

"But you got to have an opinion," snapped Paul, slamming his empty tea mug down on the trestle table. "I think it's disgusting. Worse than that, it's inhuman. It's murder, cold-blooded murder. They should round the lot of 'em up and shoot 'em."

Dean placed the lid of the urn back in position and glared at the young builder. "You mean murder them?"

Paul returned the angry stare for a moment, and then glanced over at his mate before smiling at Dean. "Yeah, you're right. Be like sinking to their level, wouldn't it? And we're more civilized than that. Give us another tea, Dean."

Before Dean could pick up the empty mug, the builder's mobile phone rang. He took it from a pocket in his cutoff jeans, mumbled a quick "Hello" and walked away from the tables to continue his conversation.

"Don't mind him," said Benny to Dean. "He gets a bit steamed up about these things."

Dean saw Frankie flash him a look that said, Leave it. He just nodded to Benny and said nothing.

Benny laughed. "That'll be his girlfriend, giving him grief about being over here. I'd better have another tea. She keeps him on that phone for hours."

3

Marcie Deveraux looked calm and unruffled as she went into a Coffee Republic and joined the line of people waiting to place their orders. But she was anxious: the secret operation she had nurtured and overseen for many months was close to being blown. And it seemed there was little she could do about it.

She took off her designer sunglasses and turned to watch the pedestrians going by outside. Nothing suspicious. She bought a latte, found a seat and took a single sip of her coffee before pulling out her Xda mobile phone and computer. Once the connection was made she didn't waste time with small talk. "I'm coming in. Five minutes."

Deveraux left the café and headed toward Pimlico. Soon she reached a street where rows of three-story town houses were grouped around their own private gardens. She pushed open a black iron front gate and walked along the cobblestone path. The red velvet curtains at the window to the left of the front door were smart and respectable. Anyone getting close enough to peer through the nets would have seen a decent three-piece suite and a good carpet. But there was no expensive TV or music system to attract the attention of ambitious housebreakers.

Three paces before Deveraux reached the door there was a low buzzing sound as the bolts slid back. She walked straight in, closed the door, and the three steel bolts returned to their locked position.

From the outside, and through the front window, the house seemed virtually identical to the others on the street. But the front room was exactly that: a front—a front of respectability and normality.

The rest of the house was different. In the hallway the paintwork was dull and faded, the carpet threadbare and the air stale and musty, as though the windows hadn't been opened in years. They hadn't. Every window in the house was screwed securely into position. They couldn't be opened. And the front room was the only place where natural light found its way into the building. The rest of the house was artificially lit. Every other window had internal shutters closed and firmly secured.

It was a safe house, manned and run by the Security Service, or MI5, the organization responsible for protecting the UK from terrorists, spies and traitors. And this safe house was special, and known to very few in the Security Service. But they were after a big fish, and Marcie Deveraux had been secretly enlisted from MI6 to help catch that fish.

She went past the stairs into a back room that opened onto the kitchen, and was immediately struck by the pungent smell of tomato soup and burned toast. Two men in their late twenties—one with long curly hair and the other wearing a blue beanie—were sitting at a long wooden trestle table. They were facing the doorway, their eyes fixed on three TV monitors on the tabletop, their ears covered by headphones.

No sound came from the monitors, or from a fourth TV

mounted above the kitchen door. The only noise was the constant hum of the internal fans cooling the monitors and the vast array of electric equipment around the room.

The long-haired man looked up at Deveraux and pulled one headphone away from the mass of curls. "He'll be here in about ten minutes, ma'am."

Deveraux nodded, aware of the admiring glances directed toward her by both young men. She was used to it: with her stunning looks and impeccable dress sense, she could have passed for a black supermodel. She glanced up at the monitor above the kitchen door. Sky News was at the House of Commons to report on Prime Minister's Questions.

The two surveillance operators went back to watching the TV screens while dunking toast soldiers into their mugs of soup. Deveraux wandered around to their side of the table, flicked some old magazines from a folding chair, sat down next to the curly-haired man and looked at the monitors.

The three black-and-white screens each showed a different location. The furthest one was split into six sections, each picking up a different area outside the house they were in.

The two closer screens were of much more interest to Deveraux. On the one in the center the four sections showed different rooms in an exclusive-looking apartment. The owner had no idea that miniature fiber-optic lenses had been fitted where walls met ceiling.

There was no one at home, but the furnishings and fittings made it obvious that this was no family residence. Every room was immaculate, nothing out of place. Almost too perfect, like a picture from a glossy, upmarket lifestyle magazine.

The closest screen showed just one room; a room that Deveraux knew very well. The hidden lens in that room was part of the wiring for one of the two wall-mounted plasma TV screens situated in one corner. The room was the office of Deveraux's immediate boss at MI6, George Fincham.

George Fincham, head of the security section; George Fincham, whose apartment was shown on the middle screen; George Fincham, the ultimate target of Deveraux's ongoing operation; George Fincham, traitor.

The Security Service had known for years that Fincham was a traitor. His activities went back nearly a decade to his time as desk officer at the British Embassy in Bogotá, Colombia. By feeding the FARC cocaine traffickers information about the operations being conducted against them he was reckoned to have amassed a fortune of around twelve million pounds, most of it hidden in foreign bank accounts. With interest, the amount was probably closer to fifteen million now.

The Security Service wanted that fifteen million, and they wanted it badly. It could be used to fund future "black ops"—the illegal, covert work the government could never officially sanction or even publicly acknowledge, and certainly never finance. Deveraux had been secretly enlisted by MI5 to recover the money, without publicly exposing Fincham as a traitor. That would be too embarrassing—for the Firm *and* the government.

As Deveraux watched the monitor, the door to the office opened and Fincham walked in. He looked his usual elegant self. Blond-haired, midforties, slick, dark blue suit and custard-yellow and red striped MCC tie. Every inch the gentleman, every inch the top civil servant. He sat at his desk and took out his mobile phone.

The curly-haired operator checked that everything Fincham was about to say would be recorded. Deveraux tapped the small speaker on the tabletop and Curly threw a switch.

Fincham punched in a number as he glanced up at the plasma screens. He was checking out the world news headlines but seemed to be staring directly at Deveraux. When he spoke into the phone his voice was crystal clear in the surveillance room. "Fran, the sighting of Watts and the boy is confirmed. I want you and Mick to link up with the other two. Plan and carry out the disposal of both Watts and the boy. But be careful—we cannot afford to mess this up in another country."

"Exactly what I was afraid of," said Deveraux, more to herself than to the surveillance operators.

Fincham ended the call, reached for the remote TV control on his desk and turned up the volume on one of the plasma screens.

Deveraux glanced up at the monitor above the kitchen door. She and Fincham were watching the same picture of the Prime Minister standing at the dispatch box, ready to answer questions about the Parliament bombing.

But before the PM had uttered more than a few words, Curly turned down the speaker so that it was just audible and nodded toward the house security screen. A man was approaching the door. "He's here."

Deveraux stood up as she heard the front door open and close and the locks slide back into place. A small, gray-haired man in his midsixties entered the room. Despite the warm spring weather his overcoat was buttoned up to the neck.

His name was Dudley. It was his surname, but he had been part of the Service for so long it could just as well have been his first name. To most in MI5 he was "Sir"; to his equals and superiors— and there were very few of those—he was simply Dudley.

"Afternoon, sir," said Deveraux.

"Good afternoon, Marcie. I don't have long."

Deveraux nodded: she was used to making short and concise reports. "Fincham has located Watts and the boy in Spain. He intends to have them both killed."

Dudley considered for a moment and then focused his eyes on the TV screen to his right. "Not exactly how you planned this, Marcie."

"No, sir. I have been monitoring their movements and I intended to bring them back at the appropriate time, when we had more to go on and Watts could be of use to us."

"Is there anything you can do now?"

Deveraux shook her head. "Since their previous escape Fincham has ensured I've had no direct involvement in the case; I argued too strenuously that they should be kept alive when they were first located. If I attempt to intervene now I risk compromising my own situation."

Dudley's shrug was philosophical. "Then I'm afraid they are lost to us, Marcie." His eyes were still fixed on the TV.

"But sir, there's still the question of who else knew Watts was operating as a K when Fincham set him up. There was, of course, Watts's old SAS commanding officer, Colonel Meacher, but as you know—"

"Fincham had him eliminated last year," said Dudley, finally turning away from the television and looking at Deveraux. "Perhaps we will have to find the answer elsewhere. Your focus must be on recovering the money. And now I really must go." He nodded toward the monitor. "The PM wants an update on the bombing as soon as he leaves the House. Anti-Muslim demonstrations outside mosques have already started. The country is scared, Marcie, and that makes our leaders very scared."

4

Señorita dice:

so wots the weather like there

Señor dice:

WOT!!!!!!!!

Señorita dice:

wot du mean wot!

Señor says:

u can not be serious!! its hot! bloody hot! 2 bloody hot! its
always hot!!!!

Danny had long since familiarized himself with MSN messaging
in Spain—here he got no time check on his monitor when he sent
or received a message. But his language, and his attitudes, remained
very English.

Señorita dice:

all right!!! theres no need 2 b an a-hole

Señor dice:

wot dyou expect??? we get a few minutes online n u ask me
about the weather

Señorita dice:

yeah, coz im not allowed 2 ask proper questions n u never
tell me anything!

Señor dice:

I cant. he won't let me

Señorita dice:

exactly!!!

Señor dice:

u tell me things then

Señorita dice:

like wot

Señor dice:

anything. something thats happened. im going crazy out here

Danny sighed as he waited for Elena to come back to him. He
was in an Internet café in Seville and this conversation was already
becoming as difficult and awkward as the last three had been.

They had an arrangement—more than that, an SOP which Fergus insisted on: Elena went online at eight o'clock British time
every morning and evening in case of emergencies. She never expected Danny to be there and so far he never had been. But every
two weeks, on a Sunday afternoon, Fergus allowed them a brief
MSN session.

Señorita dice:

all right. u remember that guy in yor year, todd hammond?
he asked me out the other day

A surge of jealousy swept through Danny's body and he felt his
face flush with anger.

Señor dice:

look, i might as well go, yor trying to wind me up now

Señorita dice:

i am not! u asked me to tell u wots happened. it happened! and anyway i said no, hes a creep. look y does it always end up like this lately? y cant we just be normal???

Normal. Danny longed to be normal again. He wanted to explain to Elena that his life had changed completely since he had last seen her. As his hands hovered over the computer keyboard he pictured the room at Foxcroft where she was sitting.

He missed Foxcroft. The harsh redbrick exterior, the creaking staircases and wheezing central heating system. The huge windows, with their broken sashes and cracked panes. He missed his old room, the posters on the walls, his computer. He even missed the garden and the lushness of the emerald green lawn after a shower of rain. He missed all the things he'd so easily taken for granted, but most of all he missed Elena.

Southern Spain was like another world where one sun-drenched day followed another. In Seville orange trees lined the wide boulevards and palm trees reached skyward. It was easy to see why the surrounding countryside was known as the dust bowl of Spain: parched brown earth, dust-blown and dry, with never a glimpse of greenery. Mile after mile of barren countryside with small, quiet towns dotted here and there.

But Danny was a city boy, born and brought up amid the noise and pace of a bustling, vibrant capital. And the longer he spent marooned in the Spanish countryside the more he yearned for the London life that already seemed so distant.

The road where Fergus and Danny ran their tea bar was newly built and sat about half a meter above ground level. Like a puckered black scar it meandered between scorched fields of ancient gnarled olive trees toward the coastal city of Huelva. In some places you could see a pair of concrete rendered gateposts with rusting iron gates standing a few meters back from the road. But there were no accompanying fences or driveways. The grand estates once guarded by the gates were long gone.

The gates were old Spain; the road itself was one of the gateways to new Spain, for it snaked its way down to the Costa de la Luz, the latest growth area for holidaymakers and second-home hunters. It was the perfect spot for a snack bar: many of the more intrepid and adventurous Brits had started choosing this route rather than the busier motorway toll roads.

Fergus had never bothered seeking permission for the business venture; he guessed no one would worry about a couple more foreigners making a few euros by the roadside. And he was right. It was too hot for complaints and arguments and filling in forms. An official from the nearest town hall had even become a regular customer; so had a couple of the local police. Fergus had operated a roadside burger bar back in Britain before he'd gone on the run with Danny. This one was different: most of the Spanish customers pulled in for coffee and a specialty hot chicken or pork sandwich cooked in garlic-flavored oil. But the Brits were attracted by the Union flag and the hand-painted sign reading: TEA. They would spill from their rented cars, desperate for a proper cup of tea, clutching new home brochures with titles like "Live the Dream."

Danny's dream was simpler. He wanted to go home. To England.

To London. But instead, every evening they returned to Valverde del Camino.

The small white house was identical to all the others in the narrow street. Each had three windows, two up and one down, with exterior shutters protected by ornate wrought-iron bars. Each house had the same carved wooden front door and a roll-down shutter for the garage.

Every night when they returned, Fergus would go through his standard antisurveillance drill: the remains of the matchstick trapped between the door and the frame would inevitably fall to the ground as proof that no one had opened it. Inside, the shutters and interior doors were always in exactly the same position as he had left them. When Fergus was satisfied the house was safe, he would park the truck, slamming down the rolling door so hard it woke up every dog in the vicinity. He didn't like creating so much noise, but he had his reasons for doing it. Then their usual evening routine would begin.

Fergus was determined to keep up his fitness levels, so most nights he completed a forty-five-minute routine of aerobic and muscle-toning exercises. Danny would go for a run, partly because he too wanted to stay fit, partly because it reminded him of his former life in England, and partly because he could escape from his grandfather, if only for a while. Then it would be a quick shower, a bite to eat, followed by a couple of hours in front of Spanish television.

Danny hated it. Endless chat shows, Spanish football, badly dubbed movies and soaps. There was even a program devoted to bullfighting. They watched it together one night and Danny stared in horror as the magnificent bull was tormented, tortured and finally brought to its knees as the matador thrust his sword into the back of its neck.

"It's disgusting," said Danny as the preening matador took the whistles and applause of the huge crowd. "I wish the bull had got him."

"It happens sometimes," said Fergus with a shrug. "And it's not just about killing. It's a bit like gladiators in the Roman arena. There's tradition, and ritual and ceremony."

"Yeah? Well, tell that to the bull," snarled Danny as he stood up and headed for the stairs. "And don't ask me to watch it again!"

They were not getting on well. After six months together they were still, in many ways, like strangers. Physically, the family resemblance was strong, but the similarity ended there. They were from different generations, different lives, different worlds.

And they argued endlessly. "I didn't ask you to come looking for me," Fergus would say when Danny moaned about the boredom and frustration of their life in Spain.

"I wish I hadn't! I'm sick to death of making tea. I was doing A levels at school—I should have a proper job!"

"You're lucky you're alive, Danny, remember that. If you're bored, read a book. Or tell me all the SOPs you can remember. You haven't done that lately."

"I don't want to know SOPs. I want a life!"

And the arguments would rage on and on. Wherever they were, whatever they were doing, Fergus remained focused on safety and security. He was quiet and secretive; it was as though he wore secrecy like a protective suit of armor. Danny was different. He could be impulsive, hotheaded, inclined to act without thinking. It didn't make for the perfect partnership, especially as

Fergus was constantly reminding Danny that he should be more like him.

Danny wanted to tell Elena all about it as he sat in the Internet café. But he didn't. He couldn't. He had his orders. His SOPs. His hands went back to the keyboard.

Señor dice:

so wot else is happening

Señorita dice:

u sure u want me 2 say

Señor says:

look im sorry 4 being a pain. go on tell me

Señorita dice:

u no who is back in court next week. he could go 2 prison 4 a long time.

Señor dice:

im sorry, i should have asked b4

Señorita dice:

don't matter. nothing u can do, nothing any1 can do, its his own stupid fault, i dont care

But she did care. Desperately. And the one person she wanted to talk about it to was Danny. But she couldn't. Fergus's rules on on-line safety applied to them both.

"U no who" was Elena's dad, Joey. Years earlier, when Elena was a small child, he'd cleared off back to his Nigerian homeland, saying he was going to make his fortune. He didn't; he just didn't come back, not until eighteen months after Elena's mum died. She had left a small inheritance for her daughter's education, and when

Elena came into the money, Joey suddenly turned up. He spun
Elena a line about investing in a fantastic moneymaking scheme
that involved exporting secondhand white goods—old fridges,
freezers and washing machines—back to Nigeria.

It was only when Danny and Fergus were safely out of the country that Elena learned exactly which "white goods" Joey was dealing in. Cocaine. And it was being imported rather than exported.
Joey and his so-called "business partner" were arrested, charged
and remanded at Her Majesty's pleasure until his trial came up.

Elena had gone through a tough six months too. She'd risked
her own life in helping Danny rescue his grandfather from the safe
house. Then she'd handed over much of her remaining cash to help
them leave Britain and start their new life in Spain. The money was
already being gradually paid back through various banks directly
into her account. But it wasn't the money that mattered.

What mattered was not knowing if she'd ever see Danny again.
And not knowing if one day the police would come knocking on
the door to arrest her for her part in the escape. And, just like
Danny, not knowing if life would ever be normal again.

Danny came back on her computer screen.

Señor dice:

i better go, he's waiting outside

Señorita dice:

yeah ok. talk in 2 weeks???

Señor dice:

hope so

Señorita dice:

i'll b here, just in case. take care

Señor dice:

u take care

Señorita dice:

bye then

Señor dice:

bye

Señorita dice:

xxx

5

Night falls quickly in southern Spain. Darkness creeps up stealthily and is suddenly there. Like an ambush.

Fergus and Danny were back at the house. The drive from Seville had passed in silence after Fergus made the mistake of asking how the online conversation with Elena had gone. Danny merely grunted, "It was crap."

Fergus said nothing more and concentrated on driving. He already felt bad enough about the way Danny's life had changed because of him.

They ate in silence and when Fergus switched on the television, Danny just sighed and went up to his room.

Fergus sat through a western movie dubbed in Spanish and then switched off the TV. He did his usual rounds, checking that the house and garage were secure, and then made his way up the stairs. Danny's room was already in darkness and Fergus knew better than to knock and say good night. His grandson was probably asleep anyway.

Ten minutes later Fergus got into bed and switched off the light. But sleep wouldn't come. He lay in the darkness, thinking. The twenty-four-hour clock at his bedside flicked over to 23:17. Two men were talking loudly as they passed by in the street below. Their footsteps faded and Fergus turned to face the wall. Soon after, he slept.

The night was still and warm, and much later a sound penetrated the wooden shutters and Fergus woke. He opened his eyes and listened. Somewhere, close by, a dog was barking. It wasn't unusual. He turned to look at the clock: 02:54. Before it had moved on to the next number he was asleep again.

Fran checked her watch. Three A.M. She stood beneath one of the small orange trees and stared across and up the road at the target house less than twenty meters away. Dull yellow light from the streetlamps barely penetrated the inky darkness. She pressed the radio button hanging from her watchstrap with a rubber-gloved finger.

"OK, let's get on with it. Fran's foxtrot."

Further down the street, on the far side of the target house, Mick heard Fran in his earpiece and began to move. The two new members of the team were watching the rear of the property, even though there was no way out in that direction. A three-meter wall completely enclosed the small backyard, but they were watching the approach routes so that, if necessary, they could give warning of any approaching third party.

The operation had been meticulously planned: the house and town had been recced on each of the four previous evenings. Fran moved forward cautiously with a square Tupperware lunch box cradled in her hands. Two large magnets were gaffered to the sides so that they stuck out just a centimeter beyond the lip of the box.

A dog was barking incessantly. Someone had spooked it. Fran made a mental note to give the new members of the team hell if it was their fault. She smiled as she got closer to the house. She and Mick had talked about this moment many times over the past six months. Revenge would be especially sweet.

They met at the garage shutter. Fran immediately stood with her back to it while Mick shone a mini-Maglite around the frame, his fingers covering the lens, leaving just enough light to check for any telltales. They couldn't allow themselves to think that Watts would leave house and vehicle completely unguarded—he was too professional for that. If there were no telltales here or inside the garage they would assume they had been left on the wagon itself.

The check of the frame revealed nothing out of the ordinary. Mick dropped to his knees, where a five-centimeter lip on the bottom of the shutter formed the seal along the concrete floor. Protruding through a hole in the center of the lip was a steel hoop, set into the floor. A padlock was securely fixed around the hoop.

Mick examined the padlock for talcum powder, or grease. If it was disturbed in any way, Fergus would know for certain that someone had tampered with it. But there was nothing. Finally Mick studied the position of the lock; when the job was over it needed to be replaced in exactly the same way. They were dealing with a man just as expert as they were.

Mick had carried out a locks recce the previous night. He placed the Maglite in his mouth and, leaning closer to cut down the spill of light, felt in the back pocket of his jeans for the two thin picks he knew would free the shutter.

The dog was still barking, and from a house not too distant came the sounds of a man and woman arguing furiously. Maybe it was their dog and neither of them wanted to get out of bed to shut the thing up. The dog seemed to join in the row, barking even louder.

Mick ignored the noise; his job was to open the shutter. If there was a problem, Fran would tap him on the shoulder and walk away. He would then get up and make off in the opposite direction.

The lock was easily defeated. Slowly but firmly Mick pulled up the shutter until he could lie on the ground and check inside with his flashlight. He concentrated on the concrete floor, looking for sand or oil that would give away their presence once they stepped inside. Even discarded rubbish or sheets of newspaper could have been placed strategically for an intruder to disturb. But again, there was nothing.

Mick pushed the shutter up a little further and slid into the garage. He placed the padlock in a pocket as Fran followed him through and then gently and noiselessly pushed the shutter back down into position.

It was a critical moment. For all they knew there could have been security cameras or a motion detector rigged in the garage. It was a risk they had to take and they would find out soon enough if they had been caught. Whatever happened, the mission had to be completed: Watts and the boy had to die. Fran had been very clear when giving her final instructions to the team. "We deal with any problem as the situation dictates."

For the moment it appeared as though luck was with them. There were no sounds of movement from inside the house; all they could hear was the muffled sound of the dog barking.

Their flashlights bounced around in the darkness, picking out little in the confined space apart from the pickup truck. Fran kept her light on the front of the vehicle and tapped Mick on the shoulder. He slowly got to his feet and she hit her radio button twice, sending only two hisses of air to the team to signify that they were in. It was quicker that way. And silent.

A Cockney voice came back to them in their earpieces.

"That you two in the garage?"

The Londoner heard two more hisses of air as an affirmative and was on the move.

"That's me foxtrot, then."

He was shifting from the rear of the house to a position at the front so that he had eyes on the garage.

Inside, Mick began feeling behind the front bumper of the Toyota and quickly found what he was searching for: a twenty-centimeter-square dust-covered metal box—a tracking device. For the past five days, until the battery finally ran down, it had sent out a constant stream of electronic beeps, one every two seconds. The device had been planted by the new members of the team. They had done their job well; young Londoners posing as builders, gradually befriending Fergus and Danny at the tea bar. Chatting casually, gaining their confidence while reporting back to London daily. And when the order to take action was given, Paul and Benny were ready.

It had been simple. Benny sipped tea and talked while Paul casually walked off with his mobile, apparently in deep conversation with his girlfriend. Planting the device took just seconds.

"Benny's in position, still clear."

Fran double clicked as she knelt down, put her flashlight in her mouth and pulled back the lid of the Tupperware box to reveal the IED. The twelve-volt battery had wires from both terminals connected to the two wires from the detonator—an aluminum tube the size of half a cigarette. It was pushed into five kilos of Semtex high explosive.

All that prevented the electric current from working its way along the wires and initiating the detonator was a thin sliver of cardboard. One wire from the battery had been cut through and the two ends wound around two drawing pins. The point of each pin was pushed into a prong of a wooden clothes-peg, with just the sliver of cardboard keeping the pinheads apart. For now. Once the cardboard was pulled free the pinheads would snap together, the circuit would be completed and bang. Big bang.

The IED was the same as those used by suicide bombers around the world; the only difference was that instead of being in a box they were usually packed into a fishing vest and worn under a coat. A length of string or fishing line would be fixed to the cardboard and fed through a coat sleeve into the bomber's hand, ready to be pulled at the vital moment.

The team had watched Fergus and Danny for the past four days. Every morning Fergus locked the front door with Danny beside him. Danny would wait as his grandfather unlocked the padlock and lifted the garage shutter. Then came the highlight of Danny's day: he was allowed to drive the wagon out of the garage and across to the opposite side of the road while Fergus pulled down the shutter and locked up.

This was Fran's chosen killing ground. She had enjoyed planning this operation, channeling her targets to their deaths, using their own repeated patterns of movement. In his final moment Fergus Watts would open the shutter, pulling the fishing line attached to the sliver of cardboard.

Fran carefully picked up the small fishing hook tied to the free end of the line curled inside the box. Slowly she fed the hook through a hole burned through one side of the box, her eyes never leaving the cardboard attached to the other end of the line.

As the hook poked through the hole, Fran slowly pulled it away from the box, allowing the line to rest on the ground. Then she placed the open top of the device against the steel shutters. The magnets clicked gently, fixing the box in the center of the shutter at about knee height.

Fran breathed deeply, glanced at the watching Mick and then hit her button.

"Ready to come out."

Outside in the darkness, Benny checked both directions. There were no signs of movement and even the barking dog had finally fallen silent.

"Clear this end. Paul?"

Paul was in a vehicle parked in the street behind the house.

"Paul's clear."

Fran double clicked and kept the fishing line still while Mick slowly lifted the shutter just enough for them to roll out into the street. Mick got to his feet but Fran stayed on the ground, winding the free line around the steel hoop concreted into the ground until there was just a little slack left. She placed the hook around the line leading up to the IED; the shutter only needed to be raised another ten centimeters for the line to tighten and pull the cardboard free.

But that was for the morning. Fran moved clear and Mick gently pushed down the shutter and replaced the padlock, ensuring it was in exactly the same position as before.

Job done, they walked away in separate directions. They would meet up again soon and return to the self-catering holiday apartment they had booked as cover. Fran smiled as she moved noiselessly down the street. Job well done: she deserved a holiday after that.

6

Fergus and Danny were still barely speaking when they emerged from the house the following morning.

Danny was first out, and as Fergus began to turn the first of the three locks that secured the front door, his grandson pulled his own set of keys from his jeans pocket. Every day it was the same monotonous routine—it was driving Danny insane. Well, today would be different: *he* would unlock the shutter. His grandfather would moan and grumble and give him another lecture about sticking to SOPs, but Danny was in the mood for a fight.

He squatted down, stuck the key into the padlock and looked up, expecting a shout, but Fergus was still concentrating on securing the front door. Danny grinned and turned the key in the padlock. It sprang open and he unhooked it from the steel hoop.

Fergus heard the metallic scraping noise and turned to see Danny squatting with both hands on the lip of the shutter. Instantly he knew it had been opened since locking up the previous night.

"*No!*" he yelled, and as Danny started to straighten and the shutter began to rise, his grandfather dived at him. He crashed into Danny's thighs and they both went sprawling to the ground.

Danny lay on the pavement, gasping and winded, as Fergus crawled on top of him, pinning him to the ground, waiting for the explosion.

It didn't come.

As Fergus looked at the shutter, now raised to just below knee height, Danny turned his head and saw the fishing line fixed to the steel hoop. He'd learned enough over the past few months to know it meant mortal danger.

"Get to the ERV," hissed Fergus. "Now!"

It was no time to argue. As soon as Fergus rolled away, Danny sprang to his feet and ran.

Fergus crawled over to the shutter, knowing only too well what was clamped to the inside. He knew too that none of the team responsible for planting it would still be in the area. They were long gone.

Fergus pulled out his Leatherman and carefully cut through the fishing line before lying down on his back and moving his head and shoulders under the shutter. Slowly he raised his hands and gently pulled the IED free. He rolled onto one side and cut the two leads attached to the battery before removing it and throwing it into the garage. The IED was safe now there was no power to initiate the detonator.

Fergus crawled all the way into the garage, then stood up with the Tupperware box in both hands and stared at the plastic explosive. It might come in useful some day.

The ERV brought back bad memories for Danny. Memories of a ramshackle, tumbledown, deserted barn in remote Norfolk.

The barn had been the last ERV where Danny had waited for Fergus. On that occasion Fergus didn't show, but Danny hadn't been alone during those six long hours. He'd had an overweight, middle-aged freelance reporter by the name of Eddie Moyes for company.

Eddie had been trailing Danny and Fergus, on the hunt for a world exclusive story about an on-the-run ex-SAS soldier, convinced it would get him back where he belonged: in the big time.

And after Fergus's capture Danny, with Elena's assistance, had talked Eddie into helping them in their attempt to rescue his grandfather. Eddie had reluctantly agreed; he couldn't bear the thought of losing his exclusive—or of the two teenagers walking into unknown and terrible danger.

So he'd helped, against his better judgment. "I'm a coward," he told them. "If it starts to go wrong you won't see my arse for dust."

Eddie had played a massive part in the rescue; if it hadn't been for him they would never have got away. But it was the last thing he ever did. Danny had watched helplessly as one of George Fincham's team put two bullets into the back of his head.

Danny was thinking of Eddie as he waited at the ERV. It wasn't the first time he'd thought about him recently. He dreamed about him often—always the same dream, a nightmare in full color.

Eddie is running from the gunman and Danny is running toward him, trying to save him but knowing it's hopeless, getting closer and closer as the pistol slowly rises in the gunman's hand.

He hears Eddie shout, "Danny, help me! Please, help me!"

And just as Danny reaches out to grab Eddie and pull him away, the pistol roars, and with his eyes wide in horror and staring accusingly at Danny, the reporter sinks slowly to the ground.

The dream never changed and Danny didn't think he would ever get over the guilt he felt for Eddie's death.

"You deal with it," his grandfather had told him many times. "You have to—you just deal with it."

But Danny wasn't like his grandfather, and after six months he still wasn't dealing with it.

The ERV was about half a mile from the house. Fergus and Danny had gone searching for a suitable place soon after moving in. A copse of scrubby trees and bushes stood at the top of a rise in a succession of stony fields. Many years earlier there might have been rows of olives—a few withered survivors were dotted here and there, but mostly the landscape was barren and bare.

From one side of the copse there was a good view down toward the town; on the other the fields slipped away to a dried-up riverbed. On the far side there were more trees and bushes and then a quiet road offering an alternative escape route. Good reasons for choosing the spot as the ERV. The middle of the copse was dense and here it was possible to remain unseen while watching for anyone approaching from any direction: another plus point—and the fact that no one ever appeared to go there made it even more appealing.

Once Fergus had settled on the copse as the ERV they had spent the next two nights bringing in and concealing escape kits. Canned food and bottled water had been stashed in backpacks, which were in turn placed in heavy-duty black plastic bags. Fresh clothes and a wad of cash were put into another black bag and the whole lot was buried just below the surface of the dry earth. The freshly dug soil was covered with leaf litter and a couple of fallen branches and the exact location marked with a large and distinct stone carried in from the field. By the time they finished it looked as though no one had been there for years.

After the drama outside the house Danny had virtually sprinted all the way to the ERV without once looking back. He arrived breathless but not panicking. They had talked about this eventuality many times and Danny knew what was expected of him.

He stayed calm, reckoning his grandfather must be OK. Danny was pretty certain that the fishing line he'd seen hanging from the shutter had led to some sort of explosive device, but there had been no explosion.

What he couldn't work out was how Fergus had known the device was there. But there was plenty to do while he thought about it. Quickly he removed the branches and leaf litter, and using his bare hands he dug into the loose soil and uncovered the black plastic bags. He took everything from the bags and then filled in the hole and replaced the leaves and branches so that the area once again looked undisturbed.

And then he sat down to wait. Six hours—that was the agreed time. He would wait for Fergus for six hours, not a second less. Danny might have moaned about his grandfather's endless lectures but now that they were back in a conflict situation he was determined to follow orders and stick to SOPs.

So he waited and watched, and the thoughts of Eddie Moyes began to return.

7

A Boeing 747 came lumbering down through the low cloud, engines whining and screaming as it made its approach to London's Heathrow Airport.

Marcie Deveraux was waiting by the fire escape on the third floor of Terminal Three's short-stay car park. The noise of the next arriving jumbo began to build and Deveraux turned and saw the brake lights of a Volvo Estate flash on as the driver realized he wasn't going to make the turn down the ramp without scratching his expensive paintwork. Brake lights switched to reversing lights. The vehicle pulled back, gears crunched and then the Volvo shot forward down the ramp. Deveraux had remained out of sight, but it wasn't to save the driver's blushes. She didn't want to be seen by anyone. She punched in a number on her Xda and put it to her ear. The call was answered quickly. "All clear," she said.

Less than a minute later a dark green Chrysler Voyager with a tinted windscreen and blacked-out windows came gliding down from the floor above. This driver knew what he was doing. The MPV stopped and a side door slid back as Deveraux stepped out from the shadows. She got in and closed the door, and as soon as she was seated the vehicle pulled smoothly away and headed down the ramps.

Dudley was in the seat next to Deveraux, still bundled up in his overcoat, despite the fact that the heat inside the vehicle seemed to be going at full blast.

"I can't pretend to be particularly impressed with Fincham's team," said Dudley. "Missed Watts again, I hear—it's getting to be a habit."

"The team is good, sir," replied Deveraux, "but so is Watts."

The vehicle cleared the car park and Dudley stared out of the window. "And I was under the impression he was just a middle-aged man with a limp." He turned to Deveraux. "Where are they now?"

Deveraux took a deep breath. "We don't know, sir."

Dudley sighed. "Why does that not surprise me either?"

"The hit should have taken place three hours ago, sir. When there were no reports of an incident, the team went back to check it out. The house was deserted but the vehicle was still there."

"Obviously. As you keep stressing, the man is good—he wouldn't be stupid enough to use the vehicle again. And what are your plans now?"

"Fincham is seething, sir. He's told the team leader that if she doesn't want to find herself working as a traffic warden she needs to complete the job within three days."

"I said *your* plans, Marcie. Tell me what *you* want to do."

The vehicle braked suddenly as the traffic ahead snarled to a standstill. Dudley leaned forward to see what was causing the holdup. There didn't appear to be any obvious problem, although in the distance a police siren began to sound.

"Well?" said Dudley, turning to look at Deveraux.

"I want to get to them first. And I have a way. I want to bring them back to finish this. I'll find out who else knows about Fincham's corruption *and* I'll get Fincham and his fifteen million."

Dudley stared at Deveraux for a long moment before he spoke again. "*Our* fifteen million, Marcie."

"*Our* fifteen million, sir."

Dudley glanced out through the window again and spoke softly. "You're a very ambitious young woman, Marcie. I admire that, and the ruthless streak; both necessary qualities in one aiming for the top."

Deveraux smiled. "Does that mean I get the go-ahead, sir?"

The smile was not returned as Dudley replied. "I will give you this chance to conclude matters. But remember this, Marcie: I can be ruthless too. Extremely ruthless."

The car phone began to sound. As the shaven-headed driver lifted it from the hands-free cradle and put it to his left ear, Deveraux noticed that half his ear was missing. It didn't seem to affect his hearing: he listened for a short while without speaking and then ended the call. With the phone still in his hand, he reached for the switch on the car radio. "I think you'll want to hear this, sir."

The radio was tuned to Five Live, but the football commentator's voice held no trace of the usual excitement associated with a Premiership match coming direct from Stamford Bridge. His quavering tones betrayed a mixture of bewilderment and fear as he tried to describe to the listeners the horrific scenes he was witnessing. "The players from both teams are standing in the center circle. Hundreds of supporters are pouring onto the field—they're desperately trying to escape the wreckage of the stands away to my right. Police and marshals are in the stands, but—"

He broke off for a moment as another voice was heard shouting, but the words were muffled and unclear amid the panic and confusion. Then the commentator came back. "I'm going to have to hand you back to the studio. The police have ordered us to clear the stadium immediately in case there's a second explosion."

8

Danny saw the figure approaching long before he knew exactly who it was, but he soon recognized his grandfather's distinctive limp. Then, when Fergus was still more than a hundred meters away, he held out both arms on either side of his body. He kept walking, arms outstretched in a crucifix position to make it absolutely clear to Danny that it *was* him.

When Fergus walked into the copse his eyes quickly took in the day sacks lying ready and the fact that the site had been restored to its original state. He nodded, satisfied that Danny had carried out his orders. "Any problems?"

"No. What about you?"

Fergus reached into a deep inside pocket of the canvas jacket he was wearing and brought out the plastic Tupperware box. "No problems—and I brought along the little present they left us." He opened the box so that Danny could peer inside. "Semtex. And don't worry, it's perfectly safe now."

Danny had been waiting four hours to ask his next question. "How did you know it was there? I've been trying to work it out—I just don't see it."

"The slats in the garage door," said Fergus, carefully looking out from the hide in every direction. "When I pull down the door at night I slam it really hard so that the slats close tightly on each other. That's my telltale sign."

"But the door was down to the ground, just like it always is."

"No, not like it always is, Danny," said Fergus. "Our visitors couldn't make any noise when they were leaving. They couldn't slam the door down, so there was no way the slats could be tightly closed. I spotted that as soon as I looked at the door, that's how I knew there was something wrong."

Danny shook his head. "If you hadn't seen it—"

"I *did,* Danny, that's all that matters. But it means we're finished here. I stuck around to see if anyone came back when the device didn't go off."

"Did they?" asked Danny.

His grandfather nodded. "Three of them. Did a walk-by a couple of hours ago. They didn't see me but I got a perfect view of them. Our friends the builders."

"Paul and Benny?"

Fergus went to one of the day sacks and pushed the box of Semtex inside. "I must be losing it—I should have spotted them. They were with the woman who killed Eddie. It means that bastard Fincham's found us."

Danny's heart sank, as the prospect of one day returning to Britain seemed further away than ever. And then an even more terrifying thought struck him. "What about Elena?" he almost shouted, expecting his grandfather to come back at him with an earful about concentrating on their own problems. He didn't.

"Just because Fincham's found us, it doesn't mean that Elena's in danger. As far as we know, he's not aware of her involvement.

But we should let her know what's happened, just in case we can't make contact for a while. You can go online to her as soon as it's safe."

Fergus delved into a backpack and took out some tins. "First we eat and get some rest. We've got a long walk ahead of us."

9

Elena didn't bother thinking up a coded screen name; she was too shocked to find Danny waiting there when she logged onto MSN.

She almost hadn't bothered. A couple of the other girls at Foxcroft were watching a DVD down in the TV room and she'd been tempted to give MSN a miss for once. But at the last moment she decided that if she missed checking in once, it would be far easier to do it a second and then a third time. It was better to stick to her usual routine, and anyway, the girls were only watching a chick flick—the stories were always the same and she'd catch up quickly enough.

Even so, she was a few minutes late logging on. And there he was. Elena speedily typed in her first message.

E says: (8:04:27 pm)
wots rong. wots happend. u ok???????????
D says: (8:04:43 pm)
don't panic. all ok
E says: (8:05:02 pm)
but uv never come online like this. somefing must
b rong
D says: (8:05:13 pm)

its ok. honest. anyway, i wanted to surprise u.

E says: (8:05:19 pm)

u have!!! but y???

D says: (8:05:26 pm)

coz im here!!!!!!!!!!!

E says: (8:05:36 pm)

wot du mean here?

D says: (8:05:48 pm)

i mean HERE. back. very close 2 u

Elena stared at the screen, hardly able to believe what she was reading.

E says: (8:06:09 pm)

ur joking, rite?

D says: (8:06:23 pm)

its no joke, im here. couldn't let u no b4, 2 dangerous.
can u get out now and I will tell u all

E says: (8:06:35 pm)

course I can. where r u? this is amazing!!!!!!

D says: (8:06:57 pm)

about 5 minutes away. meet u in 10. u no the alley two
streets behind Foxcroft, one with dead end? meet at end,
its quiet. go out back gate an be careful, don't b seen

E says: (8:07:10 pm)

i wont. going now. CANT WAIT!!!!!!!!!!!

Elena logged off and powered down her computer. As she got up from her chair and rushed to her wardrobe to get a jacket, she saw her face reflected in the mirror on the back of the door. She was smiling, grinning all over her face.

Marcie Deveraux sat in the driver's seat of a blue Nissan Almera. The vehicle was parked in the street behind Foxcroft, about thirty meters from the building. She had a clear view of the back gate; she would easily be able to trigger Elena as she headed off for her secret meeting.

In one hand Deveraux held her Xda; in the other was the small hard pen for tapping out messages on the screen. She logged off from MSN. She too was smiling, impressed at her ability to chat online like a teenager. She had been monitoring Danny and Elena's online chats for months; tonight she had played the role of Danny to perfection. Security Service technical experts had hacked into Danny's Hotmail account, allowing Deveraux to log onto MSN as Danny. She had logged on early, so that if the real Danny had attempted to contact Elena he would simply have got a message saying there were problems with the server.

Deveraux put the Xda into the glove compartment and then felt for the Sig 9 mm semiautomatic secured under her seat. She pulled out the pistol and checked there was a round in the chamber, ready to be fired. It felt comfortable in her hand.

She had her hair pulled back in a tight bun. As she tucked it under her baseball cap she saw Elena emerge from the back gate and walk quickly away. She slipped the pistol into a pocket of her bomber jacket, got out of the vehicle and closed the door with hardly a sound. She pulled the baseball cap down over her eyes and turned to follow Elena.

Deveraux had told Dudley that she was going to bring her mission to an end. Tonight was the beginning of the end.

■   ■   ■

Stamford Bridge looked like a war zone. Dudley had the collar of his overcoat pulled up around his neck to ward off the evening chill as he checked the signal on the secure mobile he held. Hastily erected arc lights illuminated the immediate area of the explosion—the stadium floodlights had been switched off to frustrate the prying television news helicopters. But as Dudley stepped through the shattered remains of plastic seating he looked up and watched as a police helicopter swooped low to chase away another heli packed with newsmen and women.

Ambulances had long since taken away the dead and wounded. Those closest had been killed or maimed by the impact of the explosion itself; others by the lethal shards of molded plastic that had flown through the air like high velocity bullets as the explosives detonated and shattered the seats. Four of the dead were not victims of the blast itself; they had been trampled underfoot as panicking supporters tried to escape.

Blue police lights on top of vehicles parked on the field flashed around the eerily quiet stadium, catching and then losing white-overalled, plastic-booted forensic officers as they picked flesh and clothing from the killing area and then placed their gruesome finds in evidence bags. Dudley watched them at work, the intermittent, flickering blue light making them look like characters in an old silent movie.

Dudley had no need of the information the forensic team would eventually discover about the explosives used in the attack: he had learned all he needed to know from watching the club's CCTV.

A teenage boy had taken his seat just before kickoff. He was wearing a black parka, unlike many of the home supporters around him, who wore their bright blue replica Chelsea shirts. The boy didn't look at the field or read the match program but kept glancing up at the nearest CCTV camera. And he was smiling.

He was lost for a few moments as the crowd stood up to cheer and chant and applaud as the teams ran out onto the field. When everyone around him retook their seats he was still smiling, and as the whistle for the kickoff sounded he stood up. With his right hand he grabbed the cord held in his left, and pulled.

The monitor screen then went black: the detonation had destroyed the camera.

Dudley was looking at the exact spot where the smiling boy detonated the IED when the mobile he was holding began to ring. He took a moment to gather his thoughts and then pressed the phone to his ear. "Dudley."

He waited for a few seconds as the private secretary making the connection passed the call on. The voice that barked out a curt "Hello?" was familiar—not only to Dudley, but to the entire country.

"Good evening, Prime Minister," he said. "I'm afraid I have bad news: Parliament was not a one-off attack. This was also a suicide bombing by a teenage boy, this time a *white* teenage boy."

The police helicopter moved across the stadium again, almost drowning out Dudley's words.

"Yes, sir, *white*. I will have a name soon. And the device used was similar, if not identical to the first. I fear the media will have a field day with this once the news gets out."

He listened to the question he knew was coming next before replying, "No, sir, we haven't discounted that. Islamic militants could still be responsible. After all, there are white Muslims. But at this stage, intelligence points us in no definite direction."

■ ■ ■

Deveraux had no need to follow Elena too closely; she knew exactly where she was going.

Elena took a left and then another left to reach the road running parallel to Foxcroft. It was a quiet street; most of the terraced houses on either side had their curtains drawn. People were home from work, settling down for another evening in front of the TV.

Deveraux gradually closed on Elena during the short walk, stalking her like a tiger waiting to pounce. Both hands were in the pockets of her bomber jacket, but the right was curled around her pistol, lower three fingers and thumb around the grip and trigger finger resting over the guard. She kept her head down as she walked.

The narrow alleyway Elena was heading for led nowhere. Once, it had run all the way through to the next street, but after a Second World War bomb had flattened a couple of houses on the far side, an enterprising builder had cleverly gained a few extra meters of garden for the new houses he erected. Now all there was at the end of the alley was a high brick wall.

As Elena turned from the street into the alley, she was hoping to find Danny waiting there for her. She couldn't see all the way to the end yet—it was too dark. There were no lights, and the spill from the lamps in the street she had left barely penetrated the gloom. Cautiously, she made her way along.

"Danny?" she whispered as she inched her way along, deeper into darkness. "Danny, you there?"

There was no answer and Elena felt a twinge of disappointment. She reached the end and then, turning to look back, saw a figure silhouetted by the light from the street at the far end of the alley.

"Danny?"

The figure gave a left-handed wave and moved silently and swiftly toward her, head still low. Elena waited: it was safer to stay where she was; they could talk there, just as Danny had said. It was only in the last seconds, as the approaching figure looked up and the right hand emerged from the bomber jacket pocket that Elena realized it was not Danny. She recognized the face, but there wasn't time to react or even say a word.

With her left hand Deveraux reached up and grabbed Elena by the back of her hair. She yanked her head back and at the same time brought the pistol up and shoved the barrel into Elena's gaping mouth. Cold metal scraped against the terrified girl's teeth; she tasted oil at the back of her throat.

"Remember me?" hissed Deveraux, forcing Elena against the wall.

Elena was too petrified to make even a sound. She stared, eyes bulging, at the face just inches from hers, remembering the woman only too well.

"Don't speak, don't move, don't do anything unless I say so. Otherwise your brains will be all over the walls. And I wouldn't want that. This jacket's new—I do *not* want it ruined. Understand?"

Deveraux relaxed the grip on Elena's hair just enough to allow her to nod.

"Listen to me, and listen good. I want Danny and Fergus back here, and you're going to make that happen."

Terrified as she was, Elena managed a tiny, defiant shake of her head.

Deveraux tightened her grip again, pulling Elena's hair so hard that it brought tears to her eyes. They ran down her cheeks and mingled with the saliva oozing from her gaping mouth as the pistol forced her lips wide apart.

"I told you to listen," said Deveraux. "If they don't come back they'll be dead within days. This way, I *might* be able to save them. And I've got an added incentive for you. Do exactly as I tell you and I'll get your father out of jail. If you don't, not only do you three die—he'll stay there until he rots. Understand?"

She relaxed her grip to allow Elena to nod again.

"Good. Now, I'm going to let go of your hair. Try to run and I *will* kill you. And you know I will—you've seen me do it before, haven't you?"

Elena nodded for a third time. She had replayed the horrific scene of the glamorous woman shooting one of the guards holding Fergus Watts many times in her mind.

Deveraux slowly released her hold on the young girl's hair, took two small steps backward and watched as Elena began to shake with fear, her legs so weak she could hardly stand. Elena suddenly realized she had been holding her breath since the moment the pistol had been shoved into her mouth.

"Breathe," said Deveraux. "Breathe deeply." It wasn't advice; it was a command. She wanted this over quickly and needed Elena to understand exactly what she had to say. "Come on, breathe, you're not dead yet."

She waited while Elena sucked in huge gulps of air. The oxygen surged into her bloodstream, making her feel light-headed. But after less than a minute the strength began to return to her limbs and she eased herself away from the wall.

"Tomorrow morning you go online, just as you always do," said Deveraux when she was certain Elena had calmed down enough to take in her instructions. "You tell Danny that he and Fergus *must* come back to the UK. And you will also tell them that you know how to get them here."

"But Danny won't be online in the morning," said Elena between deep breaths. "He never is. I was surprised to find him— you . . . I . . . I . . . I only check in case there's an emergency."

"There has been an emergency, and he will be online. I know the way Watts operates—he'll want to make contact with you."

They were both becoming accustomed to the darkness in the alley and Deveraux spotted Elena's anxious look. "What's happened? Are they—?"

"They're OK, for the moment. But it won't stay that way unless you do exactly as I say."

Elena glared at Deveraux: as her strength returned, her courage did too. "Why can't *you* go online?" she said. "You fooled me."

Fooling Elena online had been relatively simple: Deveraux had deliberately kept the MSN chat short and sweet and had told her exactly what she wanted to hear. But she knew it would be far more difficult to trick Danny, and with Fergus ever vigilant, it was too risky to attempt. Going online as herself would be even more of a risk. Fergus would almost certainly order Danny to end the conversation before it had even started, and would probably ensure that his grandson never attempted to make contact again.

The best way was through Elena, and the quickest way of gaining her cooperation had been through fear.

"I'm going to e-mail you the instructions I want you to give to Danny. They must be followed to the letter, and so must yours. When you go online to Danny, I shall be monitoring it. You tell them that you have met the woman who saved you before at the safe house. She is going to save you again. You will not go into the details of what has happened tonight. Is that clearly understood?"

Elena nodded. "But . . . but what if they won't come back?"

Deveraux's voice was cold and hard. "Not an option. They *will* come back, it's their only hope—and yours too. If not, all three of you are dead, and that apology of a father of yours stays in prison for good."

10

Señorita dice:

im so glad yor there, bin worrying all nite

Señor dice:

y? has something happened to u?

Señorita dice:

yes but im ok. u???????

Danny and Fergus had waited at the ERV until after last light, and then, carrying only their backpacks, had set out on the long walk. It wasn't the first all-night trek they had undertaken to escape pursuers, and not for the first time Danny marveled at his grandfather's ability to keep up a steady and swift pace, despite his limp.

They skirted the town and walked south, following the course of the main road but sticking to the fields. At around midnight they stopped to eat and rest for a while before moving on. An hour after first light they picked up the early bus to the coastal town of Huelva.

Among the many contingency escape plans Fergus had made

was one which involved stealing a small boat and making their way up the Portuguese coastline to some quiet little fishing port. Or even further. They had recced the harbor at Huelva and picked out potential vessels. There were plenty to choose from, particularly the small pleasure boats. Many were rarely used by their fair-weather sailor owners and sat at their moorings for a large part of the year. With any luck it would be weeks before one of those would be missed.

By nine A.M. Spanish time—eight A.M. British time—Fergus and Danny were in an Internet café and Danny was logged onto MSN. Danny's face paled as he typed in the next message.

Señor dice:

we're fine. tell me wot happened

Señorita dice:

you both gotta come back!!!!!!!

Señor dice:

wot? wot du mean???????

Señorita dice:

the woman from the safe house! i saw her. she's gonna help

u. 2nite! b4 sunrise 2morrow!

Before Danny could type in a reply, Fergus reached across and stopped him. "We need to be certain that this is Elena talking to you and it's not some kind of setup. Ask something only Elena knows the answer to."

"Like what?"

"I don't know," snapped Fergus. "Use your initiative."

Danny went back to the keyboard.

Señor says:

wot do I eat 4 breakfast?

Señorita dice:

WOT????????????

Señor dice:

just answer the question

Señorita dice:

o I get it, u don't eat anything, u don't do breakfast

Danny turned to his grandfather. "It's Elena."

Fergus nodded. "Ask her about getting us back."

Elena was ready with the instructions she had received by e-mail. As she sent them across, Fergus jotted down every word on one of the Internet café flyers he'd grabbed from the desk.

"Ask her if she's been threatened," he said as he finished writing. He wasn't expecting to get the answer he wanted and when Elena sent back her reply, he didn't get it.

Señorita dice:

can't say, u just need 2 come home

Señor dice:

u sure ur ok?

Señorita dice:

don't ask any more. just come home. PLEASE!!!!!!!!!!

Fergus had seen enough. He stood up. "We have to go, Danny. Right now."

"But we know it's Elena, and I have to tell her what we're gonna do."

"Just tell her I'll think about what she's said, but there's no guarantees, take it or leave it! Then get offline—we don't know who else is looking at that. Do it. *Now!*"

"But—"

Fergus had already walked away to pay for their drinks and the use of the PC. Danny angrily typed in his grandfather's final instruction and then reluctantly logged off without waiting for Elena's good-bye. He pushed the flimsy chair back, scraping it across the floor, and as he got up, it went crashing down.

All eyes in the café turned toward Danny, and he saw his grandfather glaring at him from the counter. He knew exactly what Fergus was thinking: Brilliant, Danny, just the way to avoid drawing attention to us.

"Sorry," he mumbled as he joined his grandfather. "But we've got to go back. For Elena. We've got to get her away from Foxcroft, so she's safe."

Fergus was staring out of the window. "Not now, Danny. You know what has to be done now and you know the drill."

Danny nodded. His grandfather was right. Someone had got to Elena; she'd said it was the woman from the safe house, but they couldn't be certain of that.

"Someone may be telling Elena exactly what to write," said Fergus. "This could be a trap; getting you two online to locate us through the machine. It only takes seconds. We need to get out. Fast. For all we know, the team could be on their way."

They took a narrow alleyway leading away from the busier part of town.

After six months of training Danny was well schooled in anti-surveillance and third-party awareness techniques. He checked behind them as they turned into a street leading toward the old town, but all the while he was worrying about Elena.

Fergus was thinking about the woman from the safe house. She had given them the chance to run six months earlier and had been prepared to ruthlessly execute one of her own team to give them that chance.

"It might not be her," he said as he walked. "Could still be Fincham himself. We don't know, and making wild guesses won't get us anywhere."

"But we are going back, aren't we?" asked Danny as they turned at another junction.

Fergus said nothing and they walked in silence for a while until they reached a wide boulevard dotted every twenty meters or so with tall palm trees and clumps of oleander. Fergus found a hiding place in bushes close to a bus stop and sat down on the ground, gesturing for Danny to join him. They would be on the next bus to arrive, wherever it was heading.

"So are we going back?" asked Danny impatiently as he sat down. "We can't just leave Elena."

"Could already be too late for Elena," said Fergus quietly. "Could be they've had what they needed from her."

Danny's skin went cold as the hairs on the back of his neck rose up. "You mean she might be . . . ?"

Fergus shrugged. "Like I said, it's pointless making wild guesses."

"But it probably is that woman," said Danny desperately. "She knows what's happened here and she wants to help us again."

Fergus didn't answer. A bright yellow bus was approaching and he stood up.

Danny grabbed his grandfather's arm as he got to his feet. "It *is* that woman, I'm certain it is. We have to trust her."

The morning sun was slanting over the tall buildings lining one side of the boulevard. The bus drew to a halt and the door swung open. Fergus looked at Danny. "We trust no one, Danny. No one."

11

George Fincham was seated at his desk, and for once the man famed for keeping his cool seemed close to losing it. He was on his mobile, but was staring up at the two plasma TV screens.

Marcie Deveraux was also looking at the TV screens. The volume was turned up on both channels, where Sky and BBC News 24 were giving details of the latest suicide bomber, now confirmed as sixteen-year-old Adam Hollis, a Catholic boy from Manchester.

Dudley had been correct in his prediction of a media frenzy on the release of the identity of the second teenage bomber. Since the first explosion at Parliament a constant stream of news pundits and armchair experts had been wheeled into every television and radio studio to fuel speculation that it was the work of Muslim extremists.

Now live TV was filled with a whole new raft of pundits. Islamic fundamentalists were still at the top of the list of suspects. After all, claimed one expert, the Islamic faith was the fastest growing religion on the planet. In the US state of Texas alone, more than half a million people had converted to Islam since 9/11. Who was to say that many impressionable British youngsters were not doing the same? But there were other theories too: everyone and everything from mad mullahs to bizarre suicide cults were getting a mention.

However, the urgency and excitement of the television voices were nothing compared to George Fincham's as he shouted into the phone. "Missing? Why didn't you tell me that before? You're saying that not only is he alive and out of our control but he has explosives? What the fucking hell are you doing over there? You may as well get your arses back here. Wait out!"

He looked at Deveraux. "I should have sent *you* to handle this. The only reason I didn't is because of your apparent obsession with allowing the two of them to live."

"Only because of the information Watts may have to give us, sir."

Fincham ignored Deveraux's comment and turned to look at a screen as the sound of the explosion burst out of the plasma's speakers. One of the news programs was replaying the fatal moment as the camera fixed for the kickoff shuddered at the impact of the bomb and then panned to the right to settle on the scene of devastation.

Deveraux picked up the remote on Fincham's desk. "May I, sir?"

Fincham nodded and Deveraux hit a button to mute the sound from both screens.

In the Pimlico surveillance house Curly and Beanie were on the early shift. They smiled as they hovered over their TV monitors; Fincham and Deveraux's conversation would now be as crystal clear as the picture they were watching.

"Way to go, Marcie," said Curly.

Steaming mugs of coffee stood untouched on the tabletop. The job could be tedious—hour after boring hour of watching nothing. But this morning the two operators had front-row seats at their very own reality TV extravaganza. Beanie checked that the recording gear was running smoothly as they listened to Deveraux speak.

"I think we should keep the team in Spain, sir," she said to Fincham. "Watts will know they planted the device. He has nothing to gain by coming back to the UK: it's too much of a risk. If I were in his situation, I would be looking for a new safe house and keeping a low profile. My suggestion is that we keep all our resources in Spain and attempt to find him. If he gets away again, we may lose him for good."

In the surveillance house Curly unwrapped a Snickers bar and dunked it in his coffee. "You tell him, Marcie."

Fincham sat back in his chair as a police helicopter flew low past his window, following the line of the river. "But where do we start?" he asked Deveraux.

"Inform the Spanish we have a warrant for their arrest; get their intelligence and police to help us find Watts and the boy."

Both surveillance operators were leaning in toward the monitor, willing Fincham to agree. "Come on, Georgie-boy," said Beanie. "Do that thing. Keep those knuckle-draggers in Spain."

But Fincham wasn't yet convinced. "I don't want the Spanish turning this into a full-scale operation."

Deveraux had worked out her plan carefully. "I don't see it as a problem, sir. We tell Spanish intelligence that it's connected with antiterrorism, the suicide bombings. Watts has explosives; Danny is another potential bomber. We explain that our people will collect the two suspects and bring them back to the UK without our respective governments knowing. It wouldn't be the first time."

"And what about their police?"

"We make it clear to Spanish intelligence that as far as their police are concerned, Watts and the boy are just a couple of criminals who need to be rounded up and thrown out of the country. That way the police help us in the hunt without knowing too many details."

Fincham stood up and went to the window stretching the length of his office. He looked out for a few moments before turning back. "All right. Contact the Spanish and keep the operation covert. Tell them we just need to know where Watts and the boy are and we will do the rest."

Deveraux nodded and got up from her chair. "Yes, sir."

Fincham reached for his mobile; then, as Deveraux headed for the door, her Xda began to ring. She looked at the phone and saw that it was the call she was expecting. Before she left the room and answered it, she glanced up at the TV screens and smiled slightly.

In the surveillance room both operators started to clap their hands, applauding Deveraux's performance.

Curly blew a kiss at the screen just before she disappeared from view. "I think she fancies me," he said with a laugh.

12

Fergus and Danny lay on the sandy earth next to the long stretch of tarmac road cutting through the remote stretch of Andalusian countryside. It was an hour before first light, the time when the night seems to be at its darkest.

Fergus had paced the distance from the road junction several miles back. They had not begun the long march until after dark and had left their final approach until Fergus stood off from the area and observed it from higher ground to ensure they were not walking into a trap. When he was sure it was safe, they moved in. Now they were in exactly the right position at exactly the right time.

The faint drone of an engine broke the silence.

"Our lift," said Fergus quietly. Right on time, as per the instructions. "When I get up, you follow, and stay directly behind me."

Danny could feel the tension as the adrenaline began pumping around his body. The moment he had dreamed of for so long had finally arrived. "Why did you decide we should go back?" he asked.

Fergus gave a short, ironic laugh. "Because basically, whichever way you look at it, we're in the shit. Sometimes, for all the training and preparation, you have to go with your gut feeling. My gut feeling is we take the ride that's been offered. At least this way we're doing something active, instead of running away. And you can't run away forever—didn't you tell me that once?"

"Yeah," answered Danny nervously.

"And anyway," said Fergus as the noise of the engine grew louder, "I never much fancied a boat trip. Always been a crap sailor. But it is a gamble, Danny—and remember, if there's more than one person in there, we don't get in. I go first, and if I push you away, you run, and you don't look back."

Fergus had a lot of experience with what they were about to do. Back in the days when he had infiltrated FARC, the drug runners had used this system to avoid government helicopter gunships, as they covertly moved their processed cocaine out of Colombia.

The engine noise was coming closer and Danny couldn't stop himself from clambering to his knees to get a first glimpse. "I can't see a thing—where is it?"

Fergus reached up, grabbed Danny and pulled him to the ground, as the roar of the aircraft's engine was suddenly just a couple of meters above them. "There!" shouted Fergus. "Stay down!"

They felt the back blast of the propeller and then heard the tires screech as they made contact with the tarmac. Danny still couldn't see the aircraft as it carried on along the improvised LS. Fergus was holding onto him tightly. "Stay behind me!" he yelled. "I don't want you walking into that propeller."

He'd seen it happen before. A lot of pumped-up, overeager young men had died needlessly by running around in the dark and getting chopped to death by the unseen propeller.

The sound of the Cessna grew louder again as it taxied back along the road toward Fergus and Danny. One wing passed over their prone bodies and then the plane turned again to face into the wind. The pilot had landed into the wind; takeoff had to be the same to obtain extra lift.

The back blast of the propeller sent sand and grit flying into the air. Danny felt it hit his face, making his skin sting, as his nose filled with the smell of aviation fuel. He shouted at his grandfather, "What's happening? Does he know we're here?"

Fergus ignored him and kept his eyes fixed on the aircraft. He knew the pilot was looking at them at that moment. The reason they had lain right next to the road was so that he could see them on his approach. If he hadn't, he wouldn't have landed.

A red flashlight began to shine. Fergus pulled Danny to his feet and, bending low, moved toward the light in a direct line. The pilot had opened the cockpit's rear door. Fergus looked inside, saw that the man was alone, then pushed Danny into the aircraft and climbed in after him. He slammed the door and slapped the pilot twice on the shoulder, indicating that they were ready to go.

The engine roared, the Cessna gathered speed and within seconds they were climbing into the dark sky. The pickup had been perfect on both sides, and Fergus nodded his appreciation; the pilot was obviously highly skilled in covert work.

In the cockpit Danny could smell coffee and see the dull glow coming from the instrument panel. He realized why the pilot hadn't needed landing lights: he was wearing NVGs. They looked like a pair of miniature binoculars, suspended about two centimeters in front of the pilot's eyes by a head harness.

A green glow was coming from the NVGs. The pilot could see as well as he could in daylight; the only difference was that everything appeared like a green negative film. And Fergus knew that the plane must also be fitted with a Nitesun light, an infrared searchlight that, together with the NVGs, had made them—and the road—perfectly visible during the landing.

Danny peered out of a window. Far below he could see clumps of lights where there were villages or small towns. In a few places vehicle headlights cut through the darkness.

The pilot took off his NVGs and switched on the aircraft's navigation lights. Bright flashes appeared at the end of each wing.

Fergus was looking down at the shape of the coastline, traced by the lights hugging the shore. They were heading north.

Without looking back, the pilot passed a flask over his shoulder. Fergus took it and began to pour out the hot, sweet-smelling coffee.

The aircraft climbed higher and Danny's spirits soared with it. He was going home. At last.

13

Elena had never had too much to say about her dad that was good. There had been too many letdowns, disappointments and broken promises, not to mention the fact that he had long ago deserted both Elena and her mum. As far as Elena was concerned, Joey Omolodon had been unfailingly consistent as a dad—he was a disaster.

But despite everything, and no matter how hard she tried, Elena had always found it impossible to actually dislike Joey. There was too much about him that was likable. He was charming, funny, confident, good-looking. True, he could drive you crazy one minute, but then he'd have you holding your sides and rocking with laughter the next. Joey was a one-off, a larger-than-life character. Or at least he had been, until going into Brixton prison.

As Elena sat in the taxi and watched her dad emerge from the prison gate, she was struck by the thought that Joey had suddenly become smaller. Shrunken somehow. He stood there clutching a plastic bag containing his few possessions, looking bewildered and disoriented.

Elena wound down the window and called, "Dad," and Joey gazed across the road, gave a little wave of recognition and a half smile and came shuffling toward the cab. He stepped off the curb and immediately leaped back as a car horn sounded and a vehicle went hurtling by.

The cabdriver laughed. "That's not unusual when they first come out. I saw a bloke get knocked down once. One minute of freedom and he walked straight under a bus." He nodded toward Joey. "Been in long, has he?"

"Mind your own business," snapped Elena as she threw open the taxi door and went hurrying across the road toward her dad.

Joey had been held in prison for four months while the prosecution case against him was prepared. Each time Elena had visited, he was sadder, more depressed and more resigned to spending many years behind bars. At first he protested his innocence to Elena; when that didn't work he said his so-called partner had set him up. Elena was having none of it: "You did it, didn't you, Dad? You're guilty," she said. And eventually Joey had just nodded.

What Joey didn't do was say he was sorry for attempting to smuggle cocaine into the country. He was saving that for the trial because he was terrified by the thought of a long prison stretch. Joey valued freedom more than anything else in life; the freedom to come and go where he wanted whenever he wanted. He'd spent his whole life doing exactly that.

Now he was walking to freedom, thanks to his daughter, and Elena thought he'd be elated, despite those first few tentative steps. But he didn't look elated.

"All right, Dad?" she asked, grabbing the plastic bag and taking Joey by the arm to lead him over to the taxi.

"Yeah, fine, babe," he answered halfheartedly. "I'm good." He didn't look good. He looked scared.

"So you're going home," said Elena brightly. "Back to Nigeria."

Joey just nodded.

"Bet you're glad about that, eh?" Elena suddenly realized that she was talking to her dad like *he* was the kid in the conversation. But she was confused; this wasn't what she'd expected.

They got into the cab and the driver pulled away. Joey stared morosely out of the window as the vehicle moved steadily through the early morning streets. "Someone came this morning, first thing," he said softly. "Just gave me a plane ticket and said they didn't want to see me back in the UK." He turned to look at his daughter. "But no one told me why they were letting me go, or why there would be no trial. Do you know what's going on?"

"No," lied Elena. "They just said you were leaving this morning and the cab would be picking me up so I could see you off."

"*They*? Who are *they*? I don't understand any of this."

Elena said nothing and they slipped into a gloomy silence as the cab moved out through the suburbs toward Heathrow. When they reached the terminal, armed police were watching at the drop-off point. The driver caught Elena's eye in the rearview mirror. "Want me to wait? It's all paid for, but I can't hang around long—the police are moving everyone on. It's this bombing business."

"I'm seeing my dad off. I'll find my own way back," she said.

Joey already had his hand on the door handle. "No, darling, you go back. You know I'm no good at long good-byes."

"But Dad—"

"No, Elena. There's two hours until my flight. You don't want to see your poor old dad in tears, do you?"

Elena could already feel tears beginning to well up in her own eyes. She brushed them away with the back of her hand and looked at the cabdriver. "Two minutes?"

The driver smiled sympathetically and nodded. "Sure."

Joey got out of the cab and waited while Elena walked around to join him. She couldn't stop herself from throwing her arms around him and hugging him.

"I'm sorry, babe," whispered Joey, his voice choking with emotion.

Elena held onto him tightly: she didn't want him to see her cry. And she *was* crying, even though she'd promised herself she wouldn't. "I'll miss you, Dad. Take care—write to me."

"Course I will, darling."

She laughed, even though she was still crying. "You won't; you never do."

Tears were rolling down Elena's face. She kissed her dad on the cheek and then turned away. She didn't look back as she walked to the cab. She didn't look back as the driver pulled away. She didn't see Joey watching the cab until it disappeared from view.

14

Danny looked down over London as the Cessna eased into its landing approach. The lights across the city and suburbs seemed to stretch away endlessly in every direction.

It had been a long and grueling flight of over one thousand nautical miles. They flew virtually the whole length of Spain and then skirted the Pyrenees and crossed into French airspace for another long haul northward, and then finally across the English Channel. Three times they landed to refuel, first in northern Spain and then twice more in France. But not once were they permitted to leave the cockpit; not even the pilot got out.

At each brief stop, air force personnel silently and efficiently approached the aircraft to carry out the refuel. No paperwork was completed, no words were exchanged; whoever was responsible for organizing the operation was high up in the food chain. Everything had been considered and prepared, right down to the bottles for peeing in. The pilot gave them each a small square cardboard box, packed with vacuum-sealed bags of food and drink—twenty-four-hour army ration packs.

Fergus grinned as he opened his. "Brings back memories," he

said, delving into the box and examining the contents. "Lancashire hot pot for dinner. What you got?"

"The same," said Danny, reading the blue words printed on the bag. "And bacon and beans, and fruit dumplings and custard."

Fergus ripped open a packet of chocolate. "This used to be pretty good. But watch out for the biscuits, they're like iron."

An incredible amount was packed into the boxes. As well as the main food rations there was soup, chewing gum, sugar, hot chocolate and carefully packed essentials like matches. There was even a small metal tub of turkey and herb pâté.

"Yanks always used to be jealous of our rations," said Fergus. "Much better than theirs."

It was the first time Danny had flown in a small plane, but the initial excitement soon turned to boredom as hour followed tedious hour. A couple of times he attempted to engage the pilot in conversation. He needn't have bothered; this was no pleasure trip, and the man at the controls was totally focused on the job in hand and was not going to be distracted.

Fergus was quiet too; his thoughts were centered on what was awaiting them when they eventually touched down in the UK.

So Danny had to settle for talking to himself or keeping his mouth shut. He chose the latter, listening to the constant drone of the engine, occasionally dipping into his rations and worrying about Elena.

They dozed for a while, but Danny was woken suddenly as the small aircraft neared the Pyrenees and was tossed about in the updrafts of air. He was scared at first, but when he saw that both Fergus and the pilot looked completely unperturbed, he sat back and enjoyed the roller-coaster ride. It was better than boredom.

They went from darkness to light and back to darkness with hardly a word spoken. But at last they were making their final descent.

Fergus knew exactly where they were headed as he looked down at the A40 streetlights burning their way west toward Oxford. "We're going into Northolt," he said quietly. "West London."

His grandson just nodded. Suddenly, with Fergus finally prepared to start a conversation, Danny had nothing to say. He was nervous; more than that, frightened. They were taking a massive gamble on coming back and had no idea what awaited them the moment they stepped out of the plane.

Fergus knew RAF Northolt well from his years in the Regiment. He had landed there many times before being driven the last few miles to what is known simply as "Northwood," the top-secret MoD control center used to conduct operations all over the world. It was at Northwood that Fergus had been given his final briefing before being sent out to Colombia as a K.

Both Gulf wars were monitored and controlled from the high security location. From the outside, all the public gets to see through the high wire fences are a few old buildings and some satellite dishes. But inside, and mostly underground in the three levels of bunkers, the complex was the closest thing Fergus had seen to the set of a James Bond movie. He remembered watching the large screens showing real-time pictures of operations in the world's trouble spots as government officials and high-ranking officers directed personnel hunched over computers.

That was in the past, when Fergus was part of it all. Now it was different. He was returning to the very nerve center of British military operations as a fugitive from the law, a wanted man.

"If there's a drama, I'll try to give you some time," he said to

Danny as the aircraft lined up on two rows of runway lights that had just started to flash. "Run toward the lights on the main road, get over the fence somehow and head left. There's a tube station after about two miles."

"But . . . but I've only got euros."

Fergus stared at his grandson and then shook his head. "Work something out."

The wheels screeched on tarmac and the aircraft bounced along the runway. Fergus checked the Semtex he had shoved down his sweatshirt. He had kept only the plasticlike high explosive and the detonator, its two wires tightly twisted together. Left free, the wires could act like an antenna, pick up radio frequencies and set off the detonator. Fergus was ensuring that the det and the HE were kept well apart at all times.

Headlights flashed in the distance and the pilot turned the aircraft away from the A40 and toward the lights. He kept the aircraft moving quickly; too fast for his passengers to attempt to jump out and make a run for it.

As they neared the vehicle, two figures could be seen silhouetted in the headlights.

Danny gripped his grandfather's arms. "They're carrying."

Fergus had already spotted the Heckler and Koch MP5s—small 9 mm machine guns—a weapon he had used himself in the Regiment. He knew that one option was already closed to them. No one outruns a Heckler and Koch.

He looked at Danny. "Forget what I said about making a run for it. You wouldn't get more than twenty meters."

The aircraft came to a standstill but the pilot kept the engine running as one of the men came toward the cockpit door. With his shaven head and most of his left ear missing he looked almost as menacing as the machine gun he was carrying. He kept the MP5 pointed at Danny and Fergus as they climbed out of the aircraft. The second man was standing midway between the aircraft and the vehicle, a Chrysler Voyager.

One Ear nodded toward the wagon, and the aircraft turned back to the runway. After the long flight in the cramped aircraft, Danny and Fergus walked slowly and unsteadily to the vehicle. As they approached, the side door slid back and Danny stooped to get in.

He stopped as he saw who was waiting inside. "Elena!"

George Fincham had a lot on his mind. As a high-ranking IB, he was rarely asked to explain his actions by a superior officer; when it did happen, it wasn't pleasant.

It had happened that day, and in a way it was hardly surprising. The teenage suicide bombers had thrown government, police and all the Security Services into a state of high alert. Manpower was at a premium and Fincham had been called in to explain why four of his most experienced operatives were apparently running around Spain "like headless chickens."

Fincham had no alternative but to admit that they were following up a lead regarding the wanted ex-SAS traitor, Fergus Watts. He knew he was on shaky ground: the recapture of traitors did not come into his remit and he had good reasons for not disclosing his personal interest in Fergus Watts.

He argued that he had acted swiftly and on his own initiative, but it didn't wash, particularly after he admitted that Watts had evaded his team and was believed to be "somewhere in Spain." Fincham was ordered, in no uncertain terms, to get the team back to the UK immediately.

He left his boss's office with the words "In future, just forget about showing initiative and stick to your own job" ringing in his ears.

Fincham was back in his own office, using his mobile to call Fran in Spain. "I am *well aware* of what I told you yesterday. There's been a change of plan—that's all you need to know. I want you and the others back here tomorrow. Be on the first plane!"

In the safe house in Pimlico, the night shift had taken over, but the two fresh operators were just as efficient at monitoring and recording every word that Fincham had spoken.

"Marcie's not gonna like this," said one as he removed his headphones and switched off the recording gear. "She wanted them out of the way."

"No bother," said his partner. "Deveraux's got it all worked out. And she's no lady to mess with."

There was no touching reunion for Danny and Elena.

Marcie Deveraux was sitting next to Elena with her back to the driver's seat. She glared at Danny and told him to "Shut up and get in the car."

He did, and Fergus followed. One Ear got behind the wheel and the second man took the front passenger seat.

"Let's go," said Deveraux to One Ear. The vehicle slowly moved off, headlights cutting through the darkness.

She turned on the interior light and fixed her eyes on Fergus. "Firstly, you need to know that I brought Cinderella here along for two reasons."

Danny expected Elena to snap back with some remark about

not being called Cinderella, but she said nothing. She was obviously scared and had been warned to keep her mouth shut.

"Reason one is to show you that she is still alive," continued Deveraux. "Reason two is to remind you that she is only alive because I am allowing it. At the moment. Got that?"

Fergus nodded.

"Good. Now listen—"

"Where are you taking us?" said Danny, unable to stop himself from jumping in.

Deveraux ignored him and kept looking at Fergus. "Haven't you taught him that he should only speak when he's spoken to?"

"Shut it, Danny," said Fergus without looking at his grandson.

"Whether or not the three of you live or die is of no concern to me," said Deveraux coldly. "If you help me, you have a chance; it's as simple as that. But it has to be fast. I've saved you from Fincham twice; we're unlikely to be as fortunate a third time. Agreed?"

Fergus nodded again. He preferred it this way: Deveraux was stating the facts; cold, hard and straight.

She took a thick brown envelope out of her handbag. "I know all about your true role as a K in Colombia, and about Fincham's activities. I aim to expose him for what he is, and you can help me do that. After all, we want the same thing: Fincham where he belongs."

The vehicle was nearing a gate. Armed MoD policemen waved them through and One Ear eased past the gate and then drew to a halt as he waited to slip into the flow of traffic.

"It's time for you to stop running, Watts," said Deveraux.

Fergus smiled. "I said that myself only last night."

"Then get your revenge on Fincham. It's payback time. Get me the names of anyone else who can confirm that you were operating as a K so that I can build my case against Fincham. I need hard proof. Fincham is a clever man—he's covered his tracks well."

"And then what, if you do nail Fincham?"

Deveraux paused as the Voyager slipped into the traffic, heading toward the A40. "Then you can start again, a free man. Danny gets his army scholarship for university and then officer training at Sandhurst; as for Elena, I've already had her father freed from prison."

Danny looked at Elena and she nodded.

"Something for everyone, you see," said Deveraux.

"And what about you?" asked Fergus. "What do you get?"

Deveraux smiled. "Job satisfaction. Now, are there any questions?"

Fergus needed time to think. He had many questions, but only one he was prepared to ask at that moment. "Your name?"

"This conversation never took place, so you have no need of my name. Elena knows how to make contact, and you will only do so when you have the information I require."

The meeting was over. Deveraux turned and tapped One Ear on the shoulder and he pulled the Voyager over to the side of the road. The door slid open and she handed Fergus the brown envelope. "Think about what I've said, Watts, but not for too long. Good night."

"What about Elena?" said Danny quickly. "Isn't she coming with us?"

Deveraux laughed. "Don't worry about Cinders. She's going home before her carriage turns back into a pumpkin. And remember this, Fincham knows nothing about her, so keep it that way."

Danny hesitated, but Elena gave him a slight reassuring smile. He smiled back, touched one of her hands with his and stepped out of the MPV. Fergus winked at Elena and followed his grandson out onto the roadside.

Seconds later the Voyager had disappeared.

15

They were surrounded by scores of lunchtime shoppers when all they really wanted was to be alone. There was so much to say, but they both knew that now wasn't the time to say it.

Elena had suggested the meeting place when Danny had contacted her online earlier. She knew that he would want to check she was OK after their encounter in the Voyager the previous night. She also knew that the MSN conversation was most probably being monitored, so she kept it brief, even though she figured that they would be expecting them to meet up anyway.

They were in a ground-floor, open-plan coffee shop inside the Lewisham shopping mall. The complex was busy, but not as busy as it would usually have been. Many people were staying at home, or at least avoiding busy places, but there was still a big enough crowd to get lost in, which was what Fergus wanted. That, and the choice of exit routes and doors leading to car parks.

Fergus was on stag, on the first floor of the shopping mall, perched uncomfortably on one of those seats specially installed in malls to ensure shoppers don't sit down for too long. He could see Danny and Elena and they could see him, and he also had a great bird's-eye view of the area.

Danny and Fergus had slept rough at the back of a Currys superstore, bedding down on a platform among the discarded cardboard and foam filler. Danny was exhausted after the long flight from Spain; he slept soundly and woke feeling a little guilty as he realized that Fergus had allowed him to sleep through instead of waking him for his stag.

They moved out early, not wanting to be discovered or tipped into a Dumpster, and went separately into a McDonald's for breakfast. They had plenty of cash: the brown envelope handed to Fergus the previous evening contained four hundred pounds in used small notes.

They sat about six tables apart while they ate and then, one after the other, went into the toilet to wash and clean up. Third-party awareness dictated that they needed to look as normal as possible: people who sleep rough don't shop in malls.

As soon as the shops were open they bought two pay-as-you-go mobile phones and some food and other gear, which they shoved into a sports bag. The phones cost £160, but Fergus said it would be worth it for secure communications. Then Danny went online to Elena.

Now they were together again, attempting to look relaxed and natural, even though they both kept their heads down to avoid the all-seeing CCTV cameras.

Fergus was watching as they leaned close together and spoke softly. As always he was being cautious. At the first hint of trouble he would get up and walk away. Danny would know it was the signal for him to walk off in another direction and for Elena to take a third route out.

The RV would be at London Bridge Station, a place they all knew well. Once they had met up there, they would have to decide whether it was safe for Elena to return to Foxcroft. They were gambling with her safety, but Fergus needed whatever information she could give them about their mysterious helper.

"She'd been monitoring our MSN talk," Elena told Danny. "Then she fooled me into thinking it was you online. I thought you were back, and when we met she . . ." She paused as the memory of the pistol roughly jammed into her mouth came back. She could almost taste it again. "I thought she was going to kill me, Danny."

She reached out and picked up the Coke standing on the tabletop. She took a long gulp, as though she was trying to wash away the taste of metal and oil.

"You okay?" asked Danny.

Elena nodded and then told him everything about her terrifying meeting in the alley: the threats, the warnings, the orders, and about Joey being released from prison. "But I couldn't tell you when I was online to you in Spain. I knew she'd be reading whatever I wrote."

Danny glanced up toward the first floor and saw Fergus look at him and then tap his watch. "What about now? How *do* you contact her?"

"She's set up a Hotmail account. Spoofed name. She said she'd e-mail me if there was anything to pass on to you and your granddad."

"What about your dad—what's happened with him?"

Elena thought back to the tearful farewell at the airport. "I saw him off at Heathrow yesterday. He'll be back in Nigeria now." She smiled. "At least I won't have to worry about him anymore. Just you."

Danny leaned even closer to her. "I've really missed you."

"Me too. And I wish we had time to talk properly. But what happens now?"

"All I know is that we're going to see one of my granddad's old mates."

"Who?"

Danny glanced up at Fergus again. "He won't say. You know what he's like—operational security, all that stuff. If I were to be caught, I might tell. Same goes for you. So basically I'll find out where we're going when I get there."

Elena finished her Coke and stood up. "You'd better go. I'll go online as usual, but remember, our friend could well be reading whatever you write."

"We thought of that," said Danny, reaching into his jacket pocket and taking out the new mobile phones. He handed one of them and a charger to Elena. "Brand-new, bought them first thing. Forget your old one—we'll use these to communicate." He passed Elena a piece of paper with a number written on it. "That's my number. Put it in your phone as soon as it's charged and then get rid of the paper. And when we speak or text, we never use our names or any other names, even Fincham's."

Elena slipped the phone and charger into her coat pocket. "Why not? No one knows we have them, right?"

"Right. But *he* said no names. There's a lot of stuff he knows that he doesn't talk about. So it's got to be no names. And forget MSN from now on, just text. That way *she* won't know what's happening."

Up on the first floor, Fergus was watching their every move. Danny stood up and glared at him. "Can't even say good-bye properly," he said. "He's always watching me."

Elena smiled. "Then I'll do it." She leaned forward and quickly kissed Danny on the cheek. "I'm glad you're back," she said and then hurried away.

16

Danny knew they were going to Hereford, the hometown of the SAS; that became obvious when Fergus handed over his train ticket. But that was all he knew. Information was being divulged on a "need to know" basis.

As soon as they boarded the intercity train at Paddington, they went into their standard antisurveillance drill. Fergus settled into one seat and Danny moved further down the carriage to find a window seat of his own.

The buffet car was out of order, so there was nothing to do but remain in their original seats all the way to Newport. Danny took the opportunity to charge his new mobile phone in one of the power points provided for laptop users. At Newport they had to change onto a local train to Hereford. They waited on the platform separately, and when they boarded the train, they took the same carriage but sat a few seats apart.

The train was quiet and Fergus was reading a newspaper. In the aftermath of the teenage suicide bombings new theories were still dominating the headlines, and journalists were searching for a connection between the two boys. But still the only link to be established beyond any doubt was that they had used identical explosive devices.

Fergus was deep in thought, considering the options the Security Services would be exploring, when he heard the voice. "I don't believe it. Watty!"

He cursed himself silently. He hadn't seen or heard the woman approach as she made her way toward the toilet; now his defenses were down. Usually, at the sight or sound of a third party approaching he would have lifted the newspaper so that it masked his face from view. But it was too late for that now: he had to try to bluff his way out.

Slowly he lifted his head and looked at the woman standing in the aisle and smiling down at him. He knew her instantly but his face betrayed no trace of recognition. "Sorry, were you talking to me?"

The woman frowned. "Blimey, I haven't changed that much, have I? You must remember me. It's Rita. Rita Stevens. You know, Gerry's wife. Or ex-wife. We got divorced; two-timing bastard made a fool of me once too often."

Rita hadn't changed much. They'd called her Lovely Rita in the old days, after the Beatles song. Now she looked a little heavier, there were a few lines etched into her face and her hair was dyed blonder and cut shorter. But Fergus remembered Rita well, and her ex-husband Gerry.

He had joined the Regiment some time after Fergus. They were never close mates, but everyone got to know Gerry and Rita Stevens. They were famed as a hard-drinking, constantly fighting husband-and-wife double act. Gerry had a reputation as a womanizer; Rita was known to have had her moments as well.

She was flashing that same old flirtatious smile as she looked at Fergus. "It must be ten years or more. You on your own? I'll get my bags and sit with you."

Fergus spoke softly: he wanted this over as quickly as possible. "I think you've mistaken me for someone else. The name's Frank."

Rita stared hard at him for a few moments and then said more quietly, "You're having me on. Aren't you?"

This time Fergus spoke abruptly, prepared to insult or offend Rita if it meant getting rid of her. "Look, I'm really not whoever it is you think I am. Now, if you don't mind, I'd like to finish reading my paper."

He turned back to the newspaper but could feel Rita's eyes boring into him for a little longer before she moved on.

Danny had heard it all, but had not looked back to draw even more attention to the brief, embarrassing meeting. But as Rita walked past his seat he heard her mumbling to herself, "Don't care what he's calling himself now, that's Watty."

When they got off the train at Hereford, Danny followed Fergus out of the station. Neither of them spotted Rita again but Danny was well aware of the damage the chance encounter could have caused. "What do we do now?" he asked as soon as he caught up with his grandfather. "She knew it was you—I heard her saying so as she went by."

"Nothing we can do," answered Fergus with a shrug. "We just hope she forgets all about it. We have to stick to our aim. The fundamental principle of any action is always to maintain the aim."

"What?" said Danny, feeling as confused as he looked. "You're just baffling me with army talk again."

"I mean we do what we came here to do."

"And what is that? It's about time you told me. I don't suppose it's for a regimental reunion."

Fergus smiled. "Of a sort. We're going to see my old mate Kev Newman. He lives here."

"Big Kev? The bloke I saw last year at the Victory Club?"

"That's him. Until you turned up, Big Kev was my only link with the old world. He's in danger too now, but he also might just come up with something I've not thought of."

"Why is he in danger?"

"Later, Danny—we need to get away from here."

Danny was suffering the usual frustration of being kept only partially informed. "So do we call to tell him we're on the way?"

Fergus shook his head. "I've thought of Kev, so someone else could have done the same thing. It's too risky to call. This is going to be a surprise reunion."

They were well away when Rita finally emerged from the station toilets with her lipstick freshly applied. She was always particular about her appearance.

She went out of the main entrance, looked around, then sighed with irritation and headed for the taxi rank. With a cigarette in one hand and a mobile in the other, she called a friend and moaned that she'd forgotten to pick her up. "Oh, and you'll never guess who I saw on the train," she added once she had finished complaining. "Watty. You know, Fergus Watts. You remember him . . ."

17

Brecon Road is one of the main drags out of Hereford. Fergus knew it well: it leads to the Brecon Beacons and the Black Mountains in Wales, the area used by the Regiment for selection courses and fitness training. It was also the road where Kev Newman lived, close to the edge of town.

It was after last light. Fergus walked casually along one side of the road; Danny was on the other, holding back by around 150 meters and watching for the moment when his grandfather disappeared into the darkness.

Smart detached houses with nice prim gardens and large estate cars in the drive lined the road. Danny had the sports bag slung over one shoulder; he kept his head down as he walked.

As Fergus passed the Wyevale Garden Center he turned left and melted into the darkness. Danny crossed the road, walked past the garden center and its parking lot and fence and slipped into the same dark area. His grandfather was three meters off the road, waiting beneath a tree. He pointed toward a black mass about ten meters further along the road. Danny could just make it out as a building. "That Kev's house?"

"No, it's our OP." Fergus started to move, using a line of bushes as cover.

Danny knew the drill without being told. Follow Fergus and do exactly as he does. If he freezes, freeze. If he kneels down, kneel down. If he runs, run, but in a different direction. They had set the ERV for outside the local swimming pool.

They carefully clambered over a crumbling brick wall into an overgrown back garden. The lights from the garden center broke through the trees just enough to expose the top half of a once grand but now derelict Victorian house.

Instead of heading toward the building, Fergus moved deeper into the garden, taking his time to ensure he made no noise as his feet found the mess of empty cans, plastic bags and ripped trash bags spewing out their rubbish.

He sat down on a pile of fallen bricks and Danny sat next to him, watching and listening for any signs of life from inside the building. They were tuning into the area; despite Danny's moans and groans over the past few months, he had learned to become a team player: together he and his grandfather looked for shadowy signs of movement behind torn curtains, or a burst of light from a window. They listened for muttering voices or a single cough.

Danny reckoned that Fergus was thinking there could be kids inside, using the house as a place to drink or take drugs; or maybe some homeless guy preparing to settle down for the night.

The minutes slipped by. Fergus was always cautious, but he seemed to be watching and waiting for an unusually long time. Eventually he leaned toward Danny and spoke softly. "OK, we're going in. If there's a drama, it's back to the ERV. OK?"

"Why did we wait so long? D'you think maybe there's someone asleep in there?"

"No," answered his grandfather. "There could be Regiment guys in there. Be very careful."

"Regi—?"

But Fergus had already started to move, and as Danny followed he was left wondering what possible reason SAS soldiers could have for holing up in a derelict house in their own town.

They edged their way up the garden and reached a smashed window. Out on the road, a couple of trucks bombed out of town toward Wales. Fergus had stopped to listen again, and as the roar of the truck engines died away, Danny could hear the sound of his own breathing.

When Fergus was ready, he climbed in through the window and waited while Danny clambered in after him. They waited for their night vision to kick in and then moved slowly from room to room over floors strewn with rubbish, checking they were the only ones in the building, and then they climbed the stairs to check the bedrooms.

The house was clear. Fergus led Danny back to the main bedroom and pointed through the window to a house across the road, where two cars and a concrete mixer stood in the drive. "That's Kev's place. I'll take first stag; you get your head down in the corner. We've got a lot to do once there's enough light to move around properly. I don't want to use a flashlight—we're too close to the road."

"But you said Regiment guys might be in here. I don't understand."

He could just see his grandfather's slight smile as he replied. "We used to use this place for OP training for Northern Ireland, that's how I knew about it. The locals never had a clue we were watching them. Big Kev always had his eye on the house over the road. It was a bit run-down then, but he reckoned it had potential."

"And now you reckon Kev's in danger. But why?"

"Because he knows I was a K. Not officially, but he knows."

"So you're gonna ask him to help us get Fincham?"

Fergus looked through the window toward the house opposite. "No, Danny, I'm not. For a start, Kev only knows because I told him everything when I got back to the UK and made contact. Which means he's in real danger because he's of no use to our friend with her so-called case against Fincham."

"What d'you mean, *so-called case*?"

"I don't believe her—not a word of it—and I've got no intention of falling in with her plan. Even if I wanted to, I couldn't."

"But . . . I don't understand."

Fergus moved over to one wall and eased himself down to the floor. "You'd better sit down for a minute."

Danny followed his grandfather across the room and sat next to him.

"There's no one else who knows, Danny, not now that Meacher is dead, I'm certain of that. Fincham's already got what he wants, he just doesn't know it. There's no one else for them to worry about."

"So why are we here then?"

"Fincham and the woman could be monitoring my closest former contacts, waiting for me to get in touch. And that's Kev. His phones could be tapped, so I have to see him to warn him. I owe him that. But then we're on our own, Danny."

18

The Pimlico safe house was starting to smell. Cleaning, tidying, washing up, taking out the rubbish—it was all part of the job for operators on a long-term surveillance. But it was the part of the job that was rarely tackled; not until there were no more clean mugs or plates, or the smell became unbearable. That moment was fast approaching.

Curly and Beanie were on the day shift and had been on duty for a couple of hours. They were sitting in front of their TV monitors. The tabletops were littered with dirty mugs and plates, chocolate bar wrappers, empty Pot Noodle containers with the congealed remnants stuck to the inside and an ashtray overflowing with stubbed-out cigarette ends. The air was thick with the mingled smell of food and stale cigarette smoke.

"About time you cleaned up a bit," said Beanie as he pushed a Pot Noodle container onto the floor to make way for his mug of soup.

"Me?" said Curly. "It's your turn. I did it last time."

"Yeah, right."

"It's those other two. They make all the mess." Curly unwrapped one of his favorite Snickers bars and dropped the wrapper onto the floor. "And their fags don't help. It's disgusting. They don't even empty the ashtray."

"We'll have a word with them."

"Yeah, it's their turn."

"Hello, Georgie-boy's got a call."

They both turned to look at the TV monitor split into four sections, each one showing a different room in George Fincham's flat.

Fincham was at home. He rarely took all the leave he was due, but occasionally he took a morning off, to make a leisurely start to the day, and to think. He had a lot to think about.

The flat looked as immaculate as ever: Fincham's cleaner had been with him for years and made sure it was always exactly as he liked it. Perfect. With nothing out of place.

Fincham had finished his late breakfast. On the mahogany table in the dining room a white bone-china coffee cup stood empty, and on a matching plate some croissant crumbs had been methodically pushed into a neat pile.

Fincham's mobile was resting on a perfectly folded napkin by the side of the plate. It was ringing.

The two surveillance operators watched Fincham move from one quarter of the TV monitor to another as he walked from the kitchen to the dining room. He answered the phone. "Yes?"

His voice was perfectly clear in the safe house and Beanie automatically checked that the recording gear was picking up every word.

"Hereford? When did this happen?"

When Rita Stevens had called her friend from Hereford Station, she set off an incredible high-tech chain of events by innocently mentioning that she had seen Fergus Watts. What Rita didn't know is that every normal, unsecure phone call, text or e-mail is sucked up by the Firm's satellite vacuum cleaners. Code name: ECHELON.

These satellites collect all the electronic information zipping around in space and send it back down to earth to be stored in huge computer mainframes. If a telephone number is programmed into the ECHELON computer, every time the phone is used, the conversation is downloaded and listened to. But, and more significantly, the computer can also be used for word recognition. Certain keywords are programmed for recognition into the ECHELON computer. Words like "bombing" or "suicide attack." Names like "Bin Laden." Or the names that Fincham had programmed in: Fergus and Danny Watts.

"Unconfirmed or not, Fran," said Fincham into his secure phone, "I want you and the team to get there now. There must be some of his generation still living in Hereford. Old friends, men he joined up with. Find them. And find Watts. I want this finished. Keep me informed."

Curly looked at Beanie. "We'd better let Marcie know about this."

19

Danny and Fergus were sitting on what remained of a sofa, facing the grime-covered bedroom window overlooking Brecon Road and Kev Newman's house. They had been busy since first light, turning the room into an urban OP, ensuring that they could look out and that no one could see in.

Some old net curtains found on the floor had been hooked above the window, pulled back at a forty-five-degree angle and held in position by bricks. From the outside, the window would look exactly as it had for years.

They stood a rotting wardrobe a meter from where the net curtain was secured to the floor and then draped a soaking wet, dark green curtain salvaged from the garden over it. This made a perfect dark background and meant that anything between the two curtains could not been seen from the outside.

The sofa was placed between the curtains, allowing Fergus and Danny to observe the target house in relative comfort.

Fergus kept his voice low as he slowly got up from the sofa. "Sort some food out while I lock up."

As Danny reached for his sports bag, Fergus went to the bedroom door, closed it and began jamming small pieces of wood between the door and the floor. "Anyone tries to come in and the stops will hold it long enough for us to go out through the window. Bit of a drop, but try and make it to the garden center, where there are plenty of people. Then go for the ERV. OK?"

His grandson nodded, hoping that a quick exit through the first-floor window would not be necessary.

Danny had done the shopping the previous day, so breakfast was a choice between Snickers and Mars bars and steak and kidney pies. Fergus wasn't bothered; he'd spent years eating junk and convenience food when on ops and had a stomach like iron. He was impressed when he saw that Danny had made ready their rations, removing all the food from its packaging and wrapping it in cling film to cut down on noise in the OP. There was bottled water to avoid the distinctive hiss of cans being opened. The plastic bottles would come in useful when they needed to pee, and in an emergency the cling film also had a secondary use. As Danny knew only too well, *everything* had to go out with them when they left. Absolutely nothing could be left behind as giveaway clues to their temporary occupation of the building.

Danny sat munching on a Mars bar while looking out at Kev's house. It was similar to the others in the row—bay windows on the ground floor and a redbrick front—but by no means identical. Big Kev was a do-it-yourself freak, and over the years, as his family had grown, his house had grown too. Now it looked as though it had more extensions than Beyoncé Knowles's hair.

Danny was looking at the roof, where two not-quite-matching dormer windows were the dominant feature. As he stared, he realized he was slowly tilting his head over to one side. "Those windows in the roof aren't straight."

Fergus laughed. "Kev never quite mastered the use of a plumb line. From what I remember, the inside's no better. He's a good bloke, though, one of the best. We spent weeks on ops like this in Northern Ireland." He paused for a moment and gazed out through the window. "Watching terrorists get together for planning meetings. Even bomb making. Last one we did together was over a chip shop in Belfast. We stank of fat for weeks."

Danny grinned. "Off on another trip down memory lane, are we, Watty?"

Fergus flashed his grandson a look, but then saw the smile on Danny's face and let it go. Besides, he'd always quite liked being called Watty; it reminded him of the old days too, when life was a lot less complicated.

"You've known him a long time, haven't you?" said Danny. "I remember him telling me."

Fergus's face clouded and he seemed to drift away with his thoughts. "We've been through a lot together. One time—"

Whatever Fergus had been about to say was left unsaid. Instead he delved into Danny's sports bag and pulled out a bottle of water.

"What?" said Danny. "One time what?"

"Nothing. It was a long time ago."

But Danny persisted. "Come on, you started telling me something. You can't just leave it."

Fergus took a drink of water. "We got into a bad contact with the IRA in Belfast. Kev was shot but I managed to drag him out and get him away in the car."

"So . . . so you saved his life?"

Fergus shrugged. "I didn't do anything Big Kev wouldn't have done for me."

They hadn't spoken like this for a long time. Ever since Danny had first met up with his grandfather, he'd found that getting him to talk about his experiences in the Regiment was as tough as pulling teeth. Now he'd learned a little more.

They sat side by side on the sofa, and as Danny thought about the special and unique bond that exists between men like Fergus Watts and Kev Newman, his feelings were mixed: awe, admiration and the slightest hint of jealousy.

He didn't like himself for feeling that way. Fergus was his only living relative, his flesh and blood. But he kept many secrets, and Danny knew those secrets could only ever be shared with someone who'd been there; someone who'd lived through the same horrors.

"So what does he do now?" he asked, trying to shake off his thoughts.

"Works for a security firm around here," answered Fergus. "But as it's Saturday—and judging by the two cars it looks as though he's at home—I'm hoping he might put in an appearance."

"Then we go and talk to him?"

Fergus shook his head. "We don't know who else is watching the house. Fincham could have people out checking anyone I know. So we watch and wait for a while." He suddenly sat up and gestured toward the house. "Here's the lad himself. He's put on weight. Lard-arse!"

Danny looked out and saw Big Kev, wearing ripped jeans and a paint-covered T-shirt, standing in the driveway with a woman.

"That's his wife, Sharon."

Kev kissed Sharon and waved her off as she got into her Mini and drove toward the town. Then he started up his cement mixer, went to the back of the house, returned with a wheelbarrow full of sand and cement and started shoveling it into the machine.

Fergus took a swig of water. "Should have guessed. Another extension."

The morning passed at about the same pace as Big Kev worked—slowly. He moved from front to back of the house with load after load of mixed cement.

"Wouldn't it be better if he had the mixer around the back, where he's working?" asked Danny after at least a dozen trips.

"Course it would," said Fergus. "But this is Big Kev we're talking about."

Sharon returned at lunchtime with a carload of packed grocery bags. She stood with one arm around the big man's waist and they chatted as they watched the mixer turn.

"They were always like that," said Fergus. "The original happy couple."

When the mix was ready, Kev went back to his barrow and Sharon disappeared into the house with her bags of shopping. Half an hour later she reappeared to call Kev in for his lunch. He'd stayed inside the house since then, although Sharon had gone off in the Mini again.

Danny had been on stag since two P.M. He had another thirty minutes to go before his two hours were up when the front door opened and Big Kev emerged. He was dressed differently: his working jeans and T-shirt had been replaced with smart chinos and a shortsleeved polo shirt, and he was carrying a golf bag stuffed with woods and irons.

As Kev walked toward his car, Danny nudged Fergus, who was

snoozing next to him on the sofa. "Heads up, Watty. He's on the move."

"Bloody hell," said Fergus as he spotted the battered golf bag. "He's still trying. I thought he'd have given that up by now."

"Is he no good at it, then?"

"He's worse than that, he's total crap. He always loved golf—must be something to do with his Scottish ancestry. He even used to take a couple of clubs and a bag of balls on ops, just in case he got the chance to practice. But he can't hit a ball straight. Never could."

Fergus smiled as he recalled golf balls being whacked in the desert, on ice-covered lakes in Norway and even *inside* an aircraft hangar the squadron had occupied for a couple of weeks in Cyprus.

"He spent a fortune on lessons, read all the books, watched the professionals, but he reckoned he never got his swing quite right. He could hit a ball for miles, but never straight. The lads used to say it was easier to dodge a bullet than one of Kev's golf balls."

Kev opened the tailgate of his Land Rover Discovery, put the golf bag inside and began rummaging around in one of the pockets.

"What's he doing?" asked Danny.

"Probably checking to see if he's got enough ammo for a whole round."

When Kev slammed the door shut, the whole vehicle shuddered. He got into the Discovery, smiling, and then drove away.

"Now what do we do?" said Danny. "Run after him?"

"No need. I know exactly where he's going."

A few minutes later, as Fergus and Danny gathered together their kit and dismantled the OP so that there were no signs of them having been there, a blue Vauxhall Vectra cruised past Kev Newman's house.

The driver pressed in his gearstick button.

"That's Mick on Brecon Road. Heading into town. Do we have any possible yet?"

Fran was crossing the river Wye, which runs through Hereford.

"That's Fran on the bridge toward the town center. There's nothing yet. All call signs, get into town and start looking for Watts until we get some Int."

20

The Thames Embankment was far quieter than usual. The fear of further suicide bombings was keeping visitors away. It was a good spot for George Fincham to talk in confidence to his trusted second in command.

Deveraux would have preferred to meet her boss in his office, where every word and look would have been recorded, but when Fincham called her and suggested they walk and talk, she could hardly refuse.

She knew all about the possible sighting of Fergus and Danny on the train to Hereford, after receiving a call from Curly at Pimlico. But as Fincham explained what had happened, she listened attentively, taking in every word as if it were all hot news to her, while making certain she gave no indication of how pissed off she was that Fergus had allowed himself to be pinged.

If Watts could be saved, he could still be useful to her to flush Fincham out and force his hand. If not, she needed to cover her own back. And there was still the fifteen million to be found.

"We haven't always seen eye to eye on this matter, Marcie," said

Fincham, after telling her he had already sent the team to seek out and eliminate Fergus and Danny. "Consequently I have, at times, not kept you fully informed of my planned course of action. I regret that now—you know how highly I regard you as my second in command."

Deveraux had decided it was time for a change of tactics with her boss. From now on she needed to know everything she could about his plans. That meant restoring his confidence in her total loyalty. "Thank you, sir, I appreciate that. But I've realized, sir, that you were right all along. We should have killed Watts when we first had him, and then taken out the boy as well."

Fincham stopped walking and stared hard at her. "But you've always been in favor of keeping them alive."

"Yes, sir, but I was wrong. I think it's time to cut our losses. Catch them again, kill them and dispose of the bodies before there's any further embarrassment."

Fincham raised his eyebrows as he considered Deveraux's words. He walked over to the Embankment railings, rested both hands on the top and gazed across the river. Deveraux joined him and they watched an almost empty pleasure cruiser cut its way through the murky brown water.

"You've taken me somewhat by surprise, Marcie," said Fincham, still staring out over the water. "I anticipated having to convince you on this one. I thought you would want to bring in Watts to question him further."

"No, sir," said Deveraux. "We tried that and it failed. And quite frankly I don't think he knows anything at all. If he did, why hide in Spain? Why not be proactive? You were right all along, sir, so let's finish it this time."

Fincham turned from the railings and smiled broadly at Deveraux. "You have no idea how delighted I am to hear you say this, Marcie. It means a great deal to me to know that I have your complete backing and can trust you absolutely."

"You can, sir," said Deveraux, returning the smile. "Absolutely."

21

Big Kev was in a bunker. He knew it well. He'd been there before, many times. It wasn't a big bunker or even a particularly deep one, but not for the first time Big Kev was thinking that he really did not like this small area of soft sand.

He'd already had two attempts at getting his ball out and onto the green. Both times he had shifted quite a bit of sand, much of it onto himself, but he hadn't troubled the ball much. It was nestling comfortably less than half a meter from where it had been when Kev first trudged into the bunker to join it.

Kev was playing alone. It wasn't that no one else would play with him; most of the club members enjoyed playing a round with Kev Newman—it was good for a laugh and it made them feel a lot better about their own game. But sometimes Kev preferred to play on his own. It gave him time to think about his game, and plenty of opportunities to search for that elusive perfect swing. He dreamed of striking the ball like his golfing hero, Tiger Woods. Kev knew he would never be even a good golfer, but once, just once, he wanted to swing the club like the Tiger.

He took a deep breath and prepared for his third attack on the ball. Both feet were planted deep in the sand and the head of his sand wedge hovered a few centimeters behind the ball. Kev focused both eyes on the little white sphere as he spoke to it. "This time you're out. On the green. Next to the flag." He reminded himself of the golden rule: "Head down, eyes on the ball, eyes on the ball."

He pulled back the club, swung down with his mighty strength and heard the sand wedge make contact with the ball. It went high into the air and Kev watched it descend onto the green and begin to roll. Quickly. It went past the flag and rolled on. And on. Without losing speed it crossed the wide green and then disappeared off the edge as it dropped into another bunker on the far side.

"Bollocks."

Danny and Fergus were close to the golf club parking lot. The walk had taken over an hour. They could see Kev's Discovery but did not approach it. Fergus wanted to avoid attracting the attention of any of the staff.

There had been a lot of activity around the entrance to the golf club. Half an hour earlier a bride and groom had arrived in a vintage Rolls-Royce, followed by carloads of wedding guests. The reception was already under way.

Danny checked his watch. "How long does it take to play a round of golf?"

"We never quite knew with Kev. He should be in just before last light, though, which is good for us."

"Then what do we do?"

"We'll wait until he gets to the last hole. We can see it from the other side of the clubhouse. I'll go and meet him and you stand off here, on stag. If there's a drama of any sort, shout me a warning and then run. The ERV is still the swimming pool. You know the drill."

A blue Transit van with LAND OF A THOUSAND DANCES MOBILE DISCO printed on the side drew into the car park and pulled up outside the clubhouse. The long-haired driver got out, went to the back of the van and hauled out a couple of heavy-duty speakers.

Fergus took Danny's arm and edged him slowly back toward the cover of some trees. He wanted to be absolutely certain that the new arrival was as genuine as he looked.

The passenger door swung open on rusted hinges and a miniskirted teenage girl slid out and stomped on high-heeled boots around to the back of the van. Her voice carried all the way across the car park. "And you start flirting with the bridesmaids like last time and you're dumped. You just stick to playing your music!"

Fergus smiled and nodded. "Looks like it'll be a noisy night."

22

Deveraux's conversation with Dudley was not proving an easy one, but she hadn't expected it to be. She was talking to him on her Xda as she walked along the northern bank of the Thames, opposite Vauxhall Cross.

"I had to tell Fincham that I fully back his decision to kill Watts and the boy on sight, sir." Deveraux couldn't hide the displeasure she felt as she spoke.

She was fairly certain that Watts, no stranger to strong-arm interrogation tactics, would keep his mouth shut if he were to be captured and interrogated—just as he had when Fincham had held him before. But Danny? He was a kid. He was bound to blurt out all he knew to save his skin, or his grandfather's. And that would eventually include all he knew about her, their mysterious helper. Three select words would be more than sufficient to give Fincham all he needed to know: young; black; woman—there were not so many of those working in the Firm.

And once the interrogation team began to get nasty, Danny would undoubtedly reveal that not only had this "young black woman" arranged their return from Spain; she had also killed one of her own team in assisting their escape from the safe house in Thetford six months earlier.

Deveraux's name would instantly go to the very top of Fincham's hit list. And once he had figured out why she was working against him—and it wouldn't take him long—he was more than likely to do a runner . . . with the money. There were still places in the world where a man with fifteen million pounds in his pocket could arrange to disappear to.

Deveraux couldn't risk that happening, but she was playing a dangerous game and she knew it. And so did Dudley. "This is becoming extremely messy, Marcie."

"Yes, sir," replied Deveraux into her mobile. "It would be inconvenient to lose Watts and the boy after expending so much energy in getting them back to the UK."

"And Fincham's team is already on the way to Hereford?"

"Probably already there by now, sir."

"But if Watts suspects he's been pinged, he may have decided not to go to Hereford at all."

"It's possible, sir, but I doubt it. He's gone there for a reason; he'll want to see it through."

As Deveraux waited for Dudley's response, she looked over the Thames to Vauxhall Cross and gazed up at the higher floors, where the heads of the Firm had their offices. She planned to move into the top floor herself one day. If this mission was a success, that move might come a lot sooner than she had expected.

"But you remain confident of recovering the money?" said Dudley at last. "Whatever happens to Watts and the boy?"

The money, thought Deveraux. Always the money. "Yes, sir,"

she said. "I will do what I can to keep them alive, but the safety and security of the mission must come first, sir."

She could hear the slight sarcasm in Dudley's voice as he spoke again. "Not to mention your own safety and security, Marcie."

"Quite so, sir, yes."

23

Fran made sure she wore a broad smile as she walked into the Queen's Arms in Hereford's town center. It was definitely more of a pint of bitter than a Bacardi Breezer pub.

"Anyone here called Kev Newman?"

Four grizzly-looking guys sitting nursing their pints looked up as Fran held up a leather wallet. "I found this outside. It's got a credit card inside and I thought he might be in here."

The four men shared a laugh. "No, love," said one of them. "He'll be at the house that Jack built, or down the golf course, *trying* to play golf."

They went back to their beer, still laughing, as Fran listened patiently to the barman explaining in great detail where Big Kev lived.

She knew perfectly well how to get to Newman's house. The Firm's intelligence cell had finally provided the information on Watts's known contacts in Hereford, including full details on his oldest mate, Kev Newman. But the information had taken a lot longer to arrive than Fran would have liked. The Security Services were at full stretch in the attempt to gather clues in the suicide bombings, and Fincham's request for information was not a priority. His team had already spent three fruitless hours in Hereford, checking out faces in pubs and cafés used by men from the Regiment, hoping to stumble across Fergus or Danny.

Now they had a lot more to go on. With a trigger on Newman's house in case he arrived home, the rest of the team were now looking at all known and possible locations. And they had Newman's driving license photograph on their Xdas.

Outside the pub she headed quickly toward her black Audi hatchback parked near the cathedral. She hit the radio button in the pocket of her jacket.

"All call signs. I have a possible location. I need the golf course checking. Who can?"

Benny was also heading back to his vehicle, a red Nissan Almera, after checking out coffee shops and a few pubs at the other end of town. He hit the button in his leather bomber jacket pocket as he kept an eye on the traffic and parked vehicles, watching for blue Discoverys.

"Benny can."

Fran was getting into her vehicle. As she pulled the door shut she hit the car button under the knob of the gearstick.

"Roger that, Benny. Paul, where are you?"

Paul squeezed the gearstick button in his silver VW Passat and the net was filled with the sounds of a truck's air brakes and a frustrated driver's car horn.

"That's Paul on the ring road and held in traffic. I got two more gyms to check out."

Fran looked at a map of Hereford as she started up the Audi. There were a couple more pubs on the edge of town that were well worth a look.

"Roger that, Paul. Mick, any change at the house?"

As soon as Mick had been given Newman's address he'd driven back to Brecon Road. He'd found the house and then immediately spotted the perfect location for a trigger on the place. He parked his vehicle in the Wyevale Garden Center car park and then slipped into the back garden of the derelict Victorian house standing alongside. He climbed in through a smashed rear window and went up to the first floor.

Using the net curtain he found lying on the floor, some heavy green curtains and an old wardrobe, he had built an urban OP. He pulled the sofa between the two sets of curtains and was now sitting in comfort, looking over at the house that Jack built.

"Mick still has the house, no change. No vehicles, lights or movement."

The big, lumbering figure of Kev Newman was just visible in the gathering gloom. Danny and Fergus could see him trudging toward them far off down the fairway. They watched as he stopped, took a golf club from his bag and then dropped the bag to the ground.

"This should be interesting," said Fergus as they saw Kev prepare to make his long approach shot to the green. He stood still for a few moments and then swung back and through. Almost immediately he hurled the club to the ground. They didn't see where the ball went, and they couldn't hear what Big Kev shouted. But when he picked up the club and his bag and moved off, it wasn't toward them, but away to the right.

Fergus laughed. "Hasn't improved much. I'll go meet him, help find his ball."

He started walking but then turned back as a thought occurred to him. "Give me your phone."

Danny pulled the new mobile from his pocket and handed it over. "Why do you want it?"

"I'd better keep this chat with Kev short, just in case. I'll give him the mobile number so he can call us. I can't remember it, and we don't have a pen to write it down."

Fergus walked off toward the fairway and Danny moved back across the car park to wait—and watch. The steady thump of disco music echoed from the clubhouse and mingled with the sounds of laughter and raised voices; the wedding party was warming up.

Kev Newman's ball had hidden itself somewhere in the deep rough. The big man had been searching for a good five minutes. The darkening sky didn't help, and he was almost ready to give up when he sensed rather than heard the approaching footsteps. He looked up, and for a moment had no idea of the identity of the man closing on him.

Then he knew. "What the—?"

"Hello, mate," said Fergus quietly. "I see you're still no better at that stupid game of yours."

Big Kev wasn't usually lost for words, but he stood staring with his mouth gaping wide.

Fergus was about three paces away when he felt something solid beneath his right foot. He bent down, picked up the ball and held out his hand to Kev. "This what you're looking for?"

Kev snatched the golf ball and then instinctively looked around to see if his old friend had been followed. "You must be bloody mad coming here, Watty. Why didn't you call me at least?"

"Too dangerous, mate."

"And you think this isn't? For me as well as you? Fergus, I've got kids, and grandchildren."

"Yeah—I've got a grandson too. The one you met. He's waiting back there for us. I've come to warn you, mate."

Kev reached down and grabbed his golf bag. "Let's get out of here." He began striding up the fairway, with Fergus at his side. "Warn me of what?"

24

Elena's laptop was, as usual, logged onto the Internet. It was in her bedroom, perched in its usual place on the desk by her bed.

But Elena wasn't there. She was downstairs, having a heart-to-heart with Jane Brooker. Jane and her husband Dave—affectionately known as Dave the Rave by the residents of Foxcroft—made sure they were on hand to talk or to listen if one of the kids in their care needed them.

They were worried about Elena. They knew her dad had left the country a lot sooner than expected but they didn't know why. But Joey Omolodon wasn't their concern. His daughter was, and she had seemed quiet and withdrawn since seeing off her dad at Heathrow. So Jane had suggested a cup of tea and a "little chat."

Elena was up for it. She liked Jane and talking to her was always good, even though this time she couldn't mention what was really on her mind.

They were in the quiet room and Jane was pouring herself a second cup of tea.

Upstairs in Elena's bedroom, a soft ping sounded on her computer. An e-mail had arrived.

. . .

Benny drove into the golf course parking lot and began to check out the vehicles.

"Stand by. Stand by! That's Newman's Discovery in the car park. Looks like a wedding in the clubhouse."

Fran immediately came on the net:

"Fran's ten minutes away. Check the course first. Look for Watts. If you see him and he's outside, take the shot. Don't wait for us, just do it. Paul, get out of that jam and back us."

Danny had watched the red Nissan Almera pull into the car park and come to a halt, just as he had watched a number of others arrive since Fergus had set off down the fairway. Every vehicle had brought late arrivals for the wedding party.

For a moment he didn't pay too much attention; he was enjoying the view from his new vantage point. It was almost last light, and in the quickening darkness he had moved to the other side of the clubhouse, where a kids' playground was situated.

Danny was perched on top of a tall slide. He still had a view of the car park and the fairway. Best of all he could now see the function room where the wedding reception was being held. He was watching the dancing and thinking to himself that if most of the people throwing themselves about to the music could actually see what they looked like they would never have got out of their seats.

Glancing over at the car again, Danny saw that the driver had gone around to the raised tailgate. Probably getting the wedding present, he thought as he turned back to his private view of the party and saw one of the bridesmaids take an inelegant tumble onto her backside.

Hunched over the rear of the Nissan, Benny was unzipping his ready bag. Inside was a bivvy bag and warm clothing in case he had to spend an unexpected night out in the country. He pushed all that aside and reached for his MP5 SD machine gun, the suppressed version of the MP5.

The two weapons look identical except for the SD's big fat barrel, which sucks up all the gases that push the round along the barrel and makes much of the bang when it escapes the muzzle. The remaining noise is the crack as the bullet leaves the barrel faster than the speed of sound. On the SD the rounds are slower, subsonic and virtually silent. Not that Benny was interested in the science, just the silence.

He pulled back the cocking handle to expose the 9 mm round that was already in the chamber. He knew that the weapon—and the pistol in his belt holster—was always made ready, but he always checked to be absolutely certain. The last thing he needed when he was close to a target was to squeeze the trigger and hear nothing more than a click.

Up on the slide, Danny suddenly noticed his grandfather and Kev Newman about thirty meters down the fairway. They had stopped and were talking quietly. Danny's attention was suddenly grabbed as the lights on the Nissan flashed. The driver had closed the tailgate and pressed the key fob to lock up. He was walking toward the clubhouse, and before he disappeared from view Danny saw that he was holding something dark down at his side. Another present for the happy couple.

Jane said all the right things about Elena and the situation with her dad. She didn't criticize Joey, or even blame him for letting

Elena down. She concentrated on the positive, saying that hopefully Elena and her dad would be able to rebuild their relationship at some time, but that for now she needed to think of herself and focus on her own future.

Elena knew she was right, and she enjoyed the chat, but right now she was finding it almost impossible to focus on anything but Danny, and what was happening to him.

Jane loved a good old chin-wag and was all set to put the kettle on for another cup of tea when Elena made her excuses, saying she had a lot of schoolwork to get through.

She hurried up the stairs, went into her room and saw instantly that she had an e-mail. She knew exactly who it was from and her eyes widened as she read the brief but chilling message.

Your friends in great danger, must leave Hereford now.
TELL THEM!

Elena's hands were shaking as she reached for the new mobile phone Danny had given her.

Big Kev was trying to help his old mate, like he always had before. He had listened in silence as they walked up the course and Fergus warned him of the twin dangers of Fincham and the mysterious woman. "I had to let you know you're in danger, mate. So that you're prepared. Like you said, you've got family."

As they neared the clubhouse, Kev stopped. "There must be some record somewhere of you being recruited as a K. If you could get to it."

"I've been racking my brains," said Fergus. "Look, I'll give you a phone number. It's secure. If you think of anything—"

The phone in Fergus's pocket began to ring. Loudly.

Danny heard the ring and as he looked toward his grandfather and Big Kev, he saw the man from the Nissan appear at the corner of the clubhouse and then dodge quickly back. And in that brief moment Danny saw that the man was carrying a weapon. He knew that shouting a warning would be wrong: he had to use the vital seconds the gunman would take to prepare for the kill. Noiselessly, he climbed down the slide.

Benny couldn't believe his luck: Watts and Newman together. He would take them both out. No problem. He stood back from the corner, put the weapon to his shoulder and took two deep breaths to steady his hold while easing off the safety catch with his right thumb. He would wait a few more seconds as the DJ inside the clubhouse talked up the next record, and when the music began he would turn and fire. Benny leaned forward into the weapon, both eyes open for a close-up aim, and waited. He could hear the murmur of conversation. Just a few seconds more . . .

Fergus knew the call was from Elena—she was the only one who had the number. He gestured to Kev that they should get off the golf course, and as they began to walk he pressed the answer call button and put the phone to his ear.

"Hello?"

Elena's voice was calm but urgent. "They know where you've gone! Get out!"

Fergus hit the end call button; he knew all he needed to know.

As he jammed the phone back in his pocket, he felt Big Kev's hand on his arm. He stopped walking and looked at his friend.

"I've got it," said Kev excitedly. "A place. Of course, a place. You need to—"

They both heard the movement from the corner of the clubhouse. As they looked toward it, they saw the gunman taking aim.

Danny crashed into Benny at full tilt. They went sprawling onto the grass, Danny's eyes watering with pain from the impact. He could see nothing as Benny rolled on top of him, but he felt the cold steel of the weapon and grabbed it. Four hands clung to the machine gun, and Benny viciously head-butted Danny as he bucked and twisted, trying to wrench the weapon free.

Fergus and Kev were too experienced to even pause with shock at the sight of the desperate struggle on the grass. Instinctively, they moved together, almost as one. Kev was still carrying the seven iron he had been using to swipe at the grass when he was searching for his ball. It was all he had to use as a weapon. He dropped his golf bag and ran, with Fergus at his side.

Before they had taken more than five strides, a dull thud came from the scrum on the grass and Fergus went down: Benny had pulled the trigger as he fought with Danny. Kev heard his friend gasp and saw him fall but he knew that his only option was to keep going, to try to stop the gunman from firing again.

"Get away from him, Danny. Get away!"

But Danny could do nothing to get away. His opponent was much stronger and had him pinned to the ground. The machine gun was between their chests and as Benny raised himself up slightly to rip the weapon free, Big Kev saw his opportunity.

Without breaking his stride, he pulled back the golf club and closed on his target.

Head down, eyes on the ball, eyes on the ball.

The swing was perfect, the elusive swing Big Kev had always yearned for. Just like the Tiger. With awesome power the club came through and hit Benny beneath the jaw. Bone shattered, blood spurted and Benny's head was almost ripped from his shoulders. His neck snapped like a straw and his body was lifted and thrown onto the grass next to Danny.

There was no doubt: he was dead.

Danny's eyes bulged as he stared up at the huge man towering over him.

"Your granddad's down, get him to the car!"

Almost too terrified to look, Danny turned around and saw the dead eyes of his attacker staring blankly at him. "It's . . . it's Benny."

Kev bent down and hauled Danny to his feet. "I don't give a shit who he was. Check your granddad—get him to the car. I'll clear up this mess."

He dug into a pocket and thrust his car keys into Danny's hands. "Come on, get a grip of yourself. And tell him PJHQ mainframe."

"What?"

"Just tell him that: PJHQ mainframe."

Music was pumping from the clubhouse. Danny wiped one arm across his blood-spattered face, then turned and ran to his grandfather. Fergus's breathing was fast and shallow and his hands were covered in his own blood as he pushed down on his jeans in an attempt to stop the bleeding. "It's the same leg; he hit the same leg."

He forced himself to sit up, grimacing with pain. "Help me up, Danny—we've got to get to the car."

Kev had Benny's body slung over his shoulders and his SD in one hand and was heading toward the car park. He had to be quick: backup could arrive at any moment. The plan was to get Benny's keys and keep hitting the fob until the right vehicle's lights flashed and the car opened up. He would dump the body in the trunk and get Fergus and Danny away in his Discovery.

Then he would worry about treating Fergus's wound, if he lasted that long. As Kev moved, with the dead weight hardly slowing him, he saw the vehicle headlights approaching.

"That's Fran at the golf course car park."

She turned her car off the road and onto the gravel.

"Where are you, Paul?"

"That's Paul two minutes away."

Fran hit the button again as her lights swept the car park and she looked for a parking space.

"Roger that. Benny, sit rep. Where are you, Benny?"

As the Audi's lights swept over the clubhouse and picked out the figure of Kev carrying Benny, Fran hit the brakes.

"CONTACT! CONTACT! BENNY'S DOWN!"

She had already retrieved her own SD from her ready bag and hidden it beneath the armrest between the rear seats. She reached back, grabbed the weapon and flung open her door.

Kev saw the door open and a figure run to the side of the vehicle. Almost immediately he felt two vibrations rattle through his body as Fran's 9 mm double tap entered the corpse slung over his shoulders. He dropped the body and brought up the SD, moving toward the headlights and looking for the attacker.

Disco lights flashed in tempo with the pumping music, casting light and shadow across the car park as Danny rounded the corner, supporting his grandfather as best as he could. In the gloom, Kev was moving toward the Audi.

"Kev!"

"In the car, move! I'll cover!"

Kev fired two rapid double taps at Fran, who was crouching beside her vehicle, but in the glare of the headlights it was virtually impossible to get a decent aim. He turned the SD on the lights and they exploded in a hail of glass.

Danny was doing his best to get his grandfather to the Discovery, with Fergus struggling to help, gritting his teeth to take the pain. As they neared the vehicle, Fergus heard the scream of an engine and saw another set of headlights turn into the car park.

"Shit! Get in the driver's seat!"

"But I can't dri—"

"You moved the truck in Spain, now move this! Get in and start it up!"

There wasn't time to argue. As Danny clambered into the driver's seat, Fergus shouted into the darkness for his friend. "Kev! Let's go!"

Kev was firing on the second vehicle as it skidded sideways to a halt and the door burst open. "Moving!"

Danny turned over the engine and heard dull pings as the Discovery took rounds. Fergus hauled himself into the backseat and thumped his grandson on the shoulders. "Get moving, toward Kev! Go! Go!"

Somehow, in halting, shunting movements, Danny edged the Discovery forward. Fergus had left the rear door open and was sprawled across the backseat. "Kev! Leave them, run for it! Come on!"

As the vehicle bucked toward the car park exit, Paul took slow and deliberate aim at the driver's side of the windscreen. The glass cracked and frosted as it took three rounds and Danny was showered with tiny shards of glass. Fear made him scream in terror, but he kept the vehicle moving.

Kev was just two meters from the Discovery. As he moved back, he was suddenly lit up by the headlights of the stationary VW. Fran held her breath. Both her eyes focused on the body mass going toward the vehicle. She shifted her point of aim to just in front of the moving body and squeezed the trigger.

The round hit Kev in the shoulder and he went down on his knees. The Discovery reached him and he made eye contact with Fergus, who was lying with one arm outstretched, ready to pull his old friend to safety, just like he had years before. But this time they both knew it wasn't going to happen.

As the vehicle passed Kev, he staggered back to his feet and began firing rounds at Fran, who was moving toward him. She had no option but to dive for cover.

From behind the VW, Paul stepped out to fire, then saw the Discovery bearing down on him. He tried to dodge away but it was too late. Danny heard a thud as the vehicle made contact.

He pulled at the wheel and turned toward the exit. Through the open door Fergus saw Kev take another round, drop his weapon and fall to the ground. The disco lights flashed off in their sequence. When they lit up the scene once more, just seconds later, he could see Fran standing over his old friend. She fired again.

Fergus reached for the door and pulled it shut. He closed his eyes and clenched them tightly together, only vaguely aware of the vehicle gathering speed. And then, through the pain, he realized his grandson was screaming at him.

"Where now? What do I do? What do I do?"

Fergus had lost a lot of blood—too much blood. Danny drove the Discovery away from the golf club and into the countryside, mainly in third gear. It was only when the streetlights ended that he realized he'd been driving without headlights. He fumbled with the steering column as the vehicle swerved from side to side. The windscreen wipers clicked into action and then suddenly the head-lights pierced the darkness.

"Stop as soon as you can," Fergus had yelled at him. "In cover!"

Danny shunted up a side road, and as he pulled the vehicle into a field entrance the engine stalled. Fergus had already pulled off his jacket and sweatshirt. "Make sure you switch off the engine, then turn the interior light on and get in the back with me."

When Danny saw his grandfather's face in the feeble glare of the small interior light he almost panicked. It was gray and the pupils of his eyes were like saucers.

Fergus threw him the sweatshirt and put the jacket back on. "You need to plug me up, stop the blood loss." He reached down and attempted to rip his jeans further apart at the point where the round had entered his thigh, but he was too weak. "Do it, Danny, rip it open."

The interior of the Discovery smelled like a butcher's shop.

Danny's hands were trembling as he tore the blood-soaked jeans apart. Fergus's thigh was like a mass of red meat where the round had torn away the flesh.

Fergus grunted in pain. "Listen to me. Rip up the sweatshirt and jam it into both the exit and the entry wounds. You've got to stop the bleeding. If I moan and shout at you, ignore me. You've got to plug the holes or I'll be going down."

"Did they kill—?"

"Yes."

There was nothing more to say. Not then.

Danny ripped the sweatshirt with his teeth and hands until he had two large pieces.

"Roll them up and pack the cavities."

Breathing deeply, and trying to ignore Fergus's curses and gasps at the almost unbearable level of pain, Danny followed his orders. The only way to stop the bleeding was to apply pressure to both entry and exit wounds. If one was left unplugged, the blood flow would only increase.

Fergus screamed again and Danny instinctively released the pressure slightly, so as to ease his grandfather's agony.

"Keep the fucking pressure on, boy!" yelled Fergus. "I told you to ignore me."

A vehicle went by, but neither Danny nor Fergus even noticed it. Danny leaned into the wounds, trying to get his weight behind the pressure he was applying with his hands as they slithered and slipped on the bloody leg.

He stayed in the same position for fifteen or twenty minutes, although it seemed like hours. His grandfather's blood had oozed all over the back of the vehicle and covered Danny's hands and arms, but the heavy flow had stopped.

"OK, get your shirt off and wrap it as tight as you can around the damage. The pressure has to stay on while you drive us out of here."

Without a word, Danny took off his shirt and bound up the wounds.

Fergus nodded. "OK, now drive! I'll tell you where to go."

At the golf club the long-haired DJ was taking a break. He walked out into the car park, with his girlfriend in hot pursuit.

"What is it with you and bridesmaids—are you incapable of leaving them alone?"

"Oh, give it a rest, Lisa, will you? I played her a record, that's all."

"You sure you didn't ask for her phone number?"

"Course I didn't. She's too pissed to remember it, anyway."

He walked further into the parking lot, leaned against the trunk of a red Nissan Almera and took out a packet of cigarettes. In the trunk of the car were two bodies: Kev Newman and Benny.

Fran and Paul, who was heavily bruised down one side of his body, had cleared up the contact as swiftly as possible. They did all they could and then left in their own vehicles. Benny's car would be picked up later.

The DJ smiled at his girlfriend. "Come here and give us a kiss."

"Not if you're lighting that fag. I don't kiss ashtrays."

The cigarette dropped to the ground and the DJ held out his arms. "Come on, Lisa, you know you can't resist me."

Lisa shrugged, then moved toward her boyfriend and they kissed. Briefly.

The DJ frowned as Lisa stepped back. "What's wrong with you?"

"I dunno, I just don't like it out here. Something about this place gives me the creeps."

27

Elena's phone was lying on her bed. She was staring at it, willing it to ring, but it remained silent.

The time had passed agonizingly slowly since her frantic warning call and she was desperate to know whether Danny and Fergus had got away from Hereford. She wanted to call again, but was trying to think tactically. If they had been captured, and Danny's phone was in the hands of Fincham's team, then redialing the mobile could compromise her own situation. Then she realized that her number was already on Danny's phone because of her previous call, as well as being in the mobile's phone book.

Elena was listening to music but it wasn't having a calming effect. The longer she sat and waited, the more anxious and frustrated she became. She had to make the call; she had to know. She switched off the music, picked up the phone and punched in the number.

Danny was gripping the Discovery's steering wheel with both hands. His driving was getting better, but not much. There was no way he could answer the phone and keep the vehicle on the road at the same time. "You'll have to get it."

The mobile was in Fergus's jacket. He had managed to prop himself up on his elbows so he could watch the road and give Danny directions. He pulled out the phone. "Yes."

"Are you OK?" said Elena, remembering the no names order. "You didn't call back and—"

"Yeah, we're fine. It's been a bit difficult to call, but thanks for the warning."

Up ahead, the road forked left and right. "Go left, boy."

Elena could hear the Discovery's engine and she also heard Fergus's instructions. "Did you say . . .? Is *he* driving?"

"No, no, of course not. He can't drive."

"I know that, but you said—"

"We're with a friend, getting out of town, and he's in the front with him." Elena was going to have to know exactly what had happened over the past few hours, but not until Fergus had worked out what their next move would be. "He . . . er . . . he sends his love."

Not for the first time Fergus was reminded that Elena, like Danny, could be very persistent. "Could I have a word with him?"

"Not now, it's not a good time, and we have to save the charge on this phone. We'll call tomorrow, early. And don't worry, we're fine." Fergus ended the call and dropped the phone onto the seat next to him.

Danny was concentrating on the road but he had listened to every word of the conversation. "I can't believe you said that."

"What?"

"That we're fine. Look at the state of us. You've got holes in your leg, we look like a couple of vampires, and you say we're fine."

Fergus grimaced as a stabbing pain shot through the wound. "We're a lot better off than we might have been. Left again."

. . .

It was way past midnight in Moscow, but George Fincham figured that fifteen million pounds entitled him to call his "broker" whenever he wanted. Not that he ever had—the more distance between them the better as far as Fincham was concerned. But this was different; this was an emergency.

Fincham was holding a brand-new pay-as-you-go phone. Using his official Firm secure phone would not be a good idea for such highly unofficial business as this. The pay-as-you-go phone would be used only once and the call would be untraceable, a system often employed by drug dealers.

Curly and Beanie had switched to the night shift and were watching Fincham on the surveillance house monitors as he pressed his password into the phone to access the credit from a twenty pound phone card. Curly adjusted the sound on his headphones and checked that everything was being taped. "This'll be interesting."

They watched as Fincham put the phone to his ear and waited. A minute passed: he was obviously going to let it ring until it was answered.

Fincham was almost ready to run; he was going to get out while he could. The news of the latest botched attempt to finish off Fergus and Danny had stunned more than angered him. Whatever he did, no matter which tactics he employed, Watts still eluded him. Fincham wasn't a superstitious man, but he was beginning to believe that fate was against him. And so he was making plans to take the money and run.

The phone in Moscow was finally lifted from its receiver and a deep, irritated voice growled a single terse word. *"Da?"*

Fincham sounded calm and relaxed as he spoke. "Good evening, it's Mr. Davies."

The man at the other end of the line paused for a moment as his sleepy brain adjusted to the switch in language. "Ah, Mr. Davies, how are you? It is very late here in Moscow."

"I apologize if I woke you, but there are certain things I need to know regarding my investments."

"I see. Then perhaps you would not mind answering some security questions?"

"Of course."

At the word "investments" the two night operators had exchanged a look, frustrated that they could hear and record only one side of the conversation.

"Fifty-six," said Fincham; then, after a long pause, "One hundred and twenty-nine."

The figures meant nothing to Curly and Beanie. They knew that Fincham was providing the numbers in a complex sum or sequence. But without knowing the other numbers, what they were hearing was useless to them.

"Ninety-three."

Fincham's "broker" was satisfied with his client's answers. "How can I help you, Mr. Davies?"

"I need to know how much of my investment I can draw immediately, or within a week at the most."

There was another pause. Fincham couldn't see the smile that spread over the face of the Russian at the end of the line. "Perhaps . . . four million. Dollars, of course. And at such short notice there would be a considerable cost involved."

"Four million dollars! But that's nowhere near my total investment!"

Curly frantically began hitting panic buttons in what he knew was a virtually hopeless attempt to get a fix on the mobile or pick up the call. "He's calling his broker! There's a broker laundering the money. Find him and we've found the cash!"

But when the broker spoke again, his words were heard by Fincham alone. "Mr. Davies, as you know, your investment covers many areas. Gold, property, oil. All guaranteed to bring you a considerable return. But for that, your commitment is long term, as we have discussed before."

Fincham breathed hard. "And if I chose to change our arrangement, call in my total investment? How long would it take?"

"Perhaps . . . six months. But there would be a significant loss of interest; probably of the capital figure also. Your business partners depend on you, just as you depend on them."

Perhaps. Perhaps. The word "perhaps" was occurring too many times for Fincham's liking. "Very well, I'll get back to you. Thank you for your time. Good night."

He ended the call and threw his mobile onto a beautifully upholstered sofa. "Bastard!"

In the surveillance house Beanie was feeling equally pissed off. He ripped off his headphones and threw them down on the tabletop. "Shit. We'll never find out who he called."

Curly was still staring at the monitors, watching Fincham pace angrily around his apartment. "Maybe there is a way," he said. "If he calls again, I reckon we'll have him. Next time we'll use ECHELON."

28

Danny was running along the tarmac road toward the fir tree plantation where his grandfather was hiding.

It was nearly first light. Fergus had told Danny to dump the Discovery in the reservoir a couple of miles down the road and then get back under the cover of darkness, before being spotted by early drivers using the route through the Brecon Beacons.

In the semidarkness he could just see the peak of the mountain behind the forestry block. This area was like nothing he had seen during his time in Spain. There, the long mountain ranges had rolled and stretched across vast areas of land. Here, everything seemed more compressed, compacted into one dark, ominous mass of towering peaks and dark forest.

He jogged off the road at a large rest area, his marker, and then jumped a stone wall and plunged into densely packed fir trees. They were like giant Christmas trees, their branches drooping almost to the ground. There was barely enough light for Danny to see where he was going. As he made his way toward the center of the plantation, he could feel the pine needles that had worked their way down the back of his neck sticking to his sweat.

Everything usable had been stripped from the Discovery before

Danny drove it away. Rubber mats laid on top of the pine needles formed a waterproof seal and the carpeting made lying down a little more comfortable for Fergus, who was still in a lot of pain.

The wound was weeping, but he knew better than to take off the sweatshirt dressings. By now scabs would have formed between the material and flesh; taking off the dressings would rip off the scabs and start the heavy bleeding again. More dressings and more pressure were needed to completely stop the blood flow from the GSW, but while Danny was away all Fergus had been able to do was use his hands to press down on his thigh.

The wind had got up and was rustling through the branches, but Fergus was being kept warm by Kev's green fleece and old Barbour on top of his own jacket. They had lost most of their kit in the contact at the golf club. All that remained was the PE and detonator, which had been in separate inside pockets in Fergus's jacket, and a little money. Very little: Fergus had been carrying the sixty pounds in notes in his jeans pocket and they were soaked in blood.

Fergus heard Danny approaching, then saw him crawling into the hide. He handed him a roll of gaffer tape taken from the Discovery. Danny could see well enough now to bind the sweatshirt dressing tightly around the wound. He started to rip tape from the roll as Fergus turned cautiously onto his side.

"Did the car sink OK?"

"Yep. Rolled down the hill no problem." Danny slowly but firmly wrapped the tape around the wound. "I reckon there's a few more down there—it sounded like it landed on another car."

Fergus grimaced as Danny fixed the tape, but then smiled as he remembered a night many years earlier. One of the rusty wrecks sunk beneath the water had belonged to Kev. They had dumped it when the battered Renault 5 failed its MOT, and then Kev reported it stolen and cashed in on the insurance. It paid for a few golf balls.

"It's deep enough," was all he said.

A vehicle pulled into the rest area, and Fergus saw Danny's anxious look. "Don't worry—it'll be the first of the dog walkers or hikers. We're at the bottom of Pen y Fan."

"You mean that mountain?"

Fergus pulled himself up against a tree trunk so that he could just see the activity going on in the rest area. "Part of selection for the Regiment is getting over the top of that thing, down the other side and back to the rest area again in under four hours. With a sixteen-kilo bergen on your back."

Danny thought back to the towering peak he had just made out as he ran back to the LUP. "Bloody hell."

A tailgate slammed, and through the branches they spotted a multi-colored sweater as a hiker went stomping off down the roadway toward the mountain path. "Some people do it for pleasure," said Fergus.

"What do *we* do now?" said Danny. "We can't stay here forever, and your leg needs attention."

"I can sort it, with the right stuff. I've been trying to think what happens after that."

Another car door slammed in the rest area: it looked as though it was going to be a busy morning on the mountain. Fergus shifted slightly to try to get himself more comfortable. "Big Kev said something to me about a place just before the contact. I didn't get the chance to ask him what he meant."

Danny suddenly remembered that Kev had barked out an order to him as he dragged him away from Benny's body the previous evening. "He said something to me—told me to tell you."

"Tell me what?"

"It was numbers or . . . or letters. Yeah, it was letters."

"Think, Danny, you've got to remember."

Danny had been doing his best to force from his memory everything that had happened during those few horrendous moments. Nightmarish images came back to his mind, but he made himself concentrate on the last few words Kev had shouted at him.

"It was something like PD or PQ. And mainframe. He said mainframe."

"PJHQ mainframe?"

"Yeah, that's it," said Danny excitedly. "That's exactly what he said. I was meant to tell you but—"

"It doesn't matter, Danny."

Danny saw his grandfather's look of disappointment. "What? What's wrong?"

"Big Kev only came up with something I'd already thought of, but it's a nonstarter."

"Why? What does it mean, this PJHQ?"

"It's Northwood, the Permanent Joint Headquarters, a command center. It's just up the road from Northolt. What Kev was saying is that there must be some record of me as a K on the mainframe computer. Evidence, Danny, official evidence. If there is anything, it makes perfect sense for it to be at Northwood, and every mainframe in the country can be accessed from there."

Danny jumped to his feet and a shower of pine needles cascaded down as he crashed into the overhead branches. "So we go there. We get in and find out what we need."

Fergus wiped pine needles from his face. "Impossible, Danny. I could never get over the Northwood fences. Even before yesterday, I couldn't have done it, but now—"

"I can do it!"

"No! No way!"

"If it's our only chance, I've got to try. And maybe Elena can hack into the mainframe. She got into Fincham's e-mail before."

"Danny, it's one of the most secure places in the UK. We'd never—"

"Look!" said Danny, bringing down another shower of pine needles. "People have hacked into the Pentagon, and NASA. If there's nothing else, we've got to *try* it."

Fergus nodded. He'd been turning over the idea of breaking into Northwood ever since the flight into Northolt, but had abandoned the idea because of the old injury to his leg. The fresh wound made any attempt by him a total impossibility. But maybe Danny could do it—if Fergus was prepared to let him try.

"We need to sort ourselves first. Cash, medical aid, change of clothes and transport. Spark that phone up."

Elena answered the call almost immediately. "What's happening?"

Danny smiled: that was Elena, straight to the point as usual.

"There's a bit of a problem—my friend was hurt yesterday. Quite a bad leg injury."

"Hurt? But last night he said—"

"I know. We didn't want to worry you."

"You're always doing this!" Elena was furious, as well as worried. "Lies, or half-truths."

"Yeah, look, I'm—"

"Just tell me what you want me to do."

"I'm going to hand the phone over now and you need to listen carefully. Got that?"

"Yes," said Elena curtly.

Fergus came on the line. "We need you to come to Abergavenny. We need some cash—quite a lot, so that we can get back and sort a few things."

"What things?"

"It's better not to talk about that now. Get the train from Paddington to Newport and change there for Abergavenny. Come out of the station, walk to the main road and turn right. There's a café in the bus station car park. You two can RV there. You won't need to stay. Get a return ticket, and we'll liaise with you again when we get back. Understand?"

"Yes."

"Text your progress. Thanks—bye."

The line went dead.

"And thank you so much for all your help and support, I don't know what we'd do without you," growled Elena as she pressed the disconnect button.

29

Even at weekends there was a virtually constant stream of traffic passing Foxcroft throughout most of the day. But there were fewer buses, and realizing there would also be fewer trains running, Elena went online and worked out a schedule for her journey.

She also needed to come up with a plausible cover story for Jane and Dave Brooker because she had made a decision of her own. If Danny and Fergus thought she was going to raid her bank account, travel all the way to Wales, hand over the cash and then wave good-bye, they could think again. She was going to help. She was going to stay, for at least one night. And anyway, if Fergus had a serious leg injury, they would need her help, not just her cash.

It wasn't unheard of for Elena to spend a night or two with one of her friends, and as far as the owners of Foxcroft were concerned she had always been completely truthful. She was their model resident: straight-A student at school, polite, responsible, considerate, mature. She had coped with the disappearance of her best friend Danny six months earlier and had philosophically accepted that her failure of a father had let her down yet again and been packed off back to Nigeria.

And besides, Elena was at an age when she had to be allowed

some freedom. It was part of growing up, and Jane and Dave had to judge when they could allow the kids in their care to start preparing for their life after Foxcroft. With some kids that could be a big problem, but not with Elena. She was straight, honest and trustworthy.

So when Elena told Jane a pack of lies, Jane believed every word.

"I'm staying with Alice tonight, maybe tomorrow as well. We're working on a project together and it's easier at her place than here. Her mum says it's OK."

Jane smiled. She'd met Elena's school friend Alice and liked her. "That's fine, love. Should I call Alice's mum, just to have a word?"

Elena arched her eyebrows as if to say, Jane, please! Don't embarrass me. Don't treat me like I'm a child.

It was a risk. If Jane made the call and discovered that no such arrangement had been made, then Elena's credibility would be blown for good. But Jane trusted Elena. Completely.

"You have a lovely time. And call me this evening."

"I will. Thanks, Jane."

Elena felt bad as she went back to her room, but lying had been her only option. She threw some clothes into a bag, and then slipped in her laptop as well, knowing she had to be contactable on the Internet. She made sure she had her building society debit card, and then hurried downstairs and went out to catch her bus.

As soon as she stepped out of the front door, she was followed.

Elena had no reason to believe anyone would be tailing her. If the woman—whose name she still didn't know—wanted to make contact it would be done by e-mail. That was the arrangement, and Elena had checked her messages before leaving. There had been nothing. So she walked toward the bus stop thinking about Danny and meeting up with him in a few hours' time.

As she reached the bus stop she felt the hand on her shoulder. She froze, and the memory of her terrifying encounter in the alley behind Foxcroft came back to her. At least here in public nothing like that could happen: although there was no one at the bus stop, there were people around and cars passing, and for a moment Elena thought of calling out or running back to Foxcroft. But that would only lead to unwanted questions, and at the very least a delay in getting to Danny.

Slowly Elena turned around and her eyes widened in shock.

"Hello, babe."

It was cold in the forestry plantation. The wind had grown stronger and was whipping through the fir trees. Danny was wearing Kev's Barbour and Fergus had the green fleece around his shoulders.

"We ought to talk about it."

"What?"

"You know what I mean, Danny."

Danny felt the fear return. "Kev?"

Fergus nodded. "I know you're thinking about him; so am I. And I saw what happened."

"I don't want to know the details."

"I wasn't going to give you the details. But we do need to—"

"Deal with it?" snapped Danny. "That's your answer to everything. Something terrible happens, someone gets killed, and you just say deal with it! Well I can't, not this time!"

Danny had tears in his eyes. He was hurting, and angry, and afraid. And as much as he mourned the death of Big Kev, one look at his grandfather lying slumped against the tree, his face gray, his leg covered with congealed blood, told Danny that it could just as easily have been Fergus who had died.

And Danny couldn't bear the thought of that. The events of the last few hours had shown him just how much his grandfather meant to him now. But that wasn't easy to explain, not to a man like Fergus Watts; a man who seemed to have spent his entire life keeping his emotions in check.

Danny stood up. "I'd better get going; it'll take a while to get to Abergavenny."

"Wait," said Fergus, pushing himself up a little further. "We've never really talked about this sort of stuff—and you're right, I'm not great at it. But Kev was a good mate; you'll be lucky if you find two or three as good in your whole life. He was the last of mine, and I'll miss him. And I've got to live with the fact that if we hadn't turned up, he'd probably be starting another game of golf right now."

"But how do you? How can you live with it?"

Fergus paused before answering. "I'll think about the laughs we had. The good times. And I'll remember that he died to save us. Paid me back for saving him all those years ago."

Danny couldn't hold back what he wanted to say. "And what if it had been you? I'm sorry about Kev, really sorry, but . . . but I don't want you to die. It took me seventeen years to find you and . . . and . . ."

"I know, Danny," said Fergus gently. "And I'm not planning on dying just yet. I don't want to lose you either . . .

"You'd better get going," he added after a long pause. "And be careful."

"I will."

As Danny turned to go, his grandfather wiped away a single tear that was rolling down his cheek. He felt embarrassed, stupid, and he was glad that Danny hadn't seen it. Fergus Watts didn't do this sort of thing. He had no idea who the tear was for. For Big Kev? For the grandson he had come to love? Or for himself?

He heard Danny moving through the branches and smiled. "You won't get rid of me yet," he whispered.

Elena was desperate to get rid of her dad. "No way! You are *not* coming with me!"

"But I got nowhere else to go, darling, and no money."

Once Elena had recovered from the shock of seeing Joey standing there beaming at her, they had moved into the bus shelter, and they had been arguing for a full five minutes since then.

"You should have gone back—I thought you *had* gone."

Joey sighed. "Yeah, well, there's something I didn't quite get around to telling you about, darling. I can't go back to Nigeria—bit of a misunderstanding with the police."

"What did you do?"

"Some money went missing, quite a lot of money. It was nothing to do with me, darling, honest. But once you get a reputation like mine—"

"And a *record* like yours!"

Joey breathed hard. He'd been living rough for the past couple of nights and it didn't suit him. He was tired, hungry and broke, and he was certainly no Fergus Watts. Prison had been bad enough, but surviving out in the open, sleeping on benches—it was more than he could handle.

"The truth is, babe, if I go back home they'll lock me up and throw away the key. And prisons in Nigeria are a whole lot tougher than here. I won't survive."

Elena looked at her watch. She was going to be late.

"Where is it you're going anyway, darling?" asked Joey.

There wasn't time to think up a convincing lie. "To see my friend, Danny. He needs my help."

"Him? Again? That boy's always in trouble."

"Yeah. Like you."

"Let me come—I helped you before, I can do it again. Your dad's always here for you, darling."

"No, Dad, no way. No, no, *no*!"

30

Considering everything that had happened to him in the past twenty-four hours, Danny didn't look too bad, as long as no one studied him closely. He had washed his hands, arms, face and hair in an icy-cold Welsh mountain stream and had Kev's Barbour done up over his own clothes to cover the dried bloodstains. The sixty pounds in notes had also had a wash and was now drying in Danny's underpants, next to his skin. Fergus had told him that was the way he used to dry his socks when out in the field.

Danny was waiting across the road from the car park café, standing in the doorway of a closed-down antiques shop. From there he had a good view of everyone leaving the station. He was feeling weary after a seven-mile trek to Brecon, where he had caught the bus for the forty-five-minute journey to Abergavenny.

He took the mobile from a pocket in the Barbour and reread the text he had received a few minutes earlier:

B THERE IN 10

He was looking forward to seeing Elena, even though their meeting would have to be brief. At least they would have time to go to the superstore he had spotted to buy some new clothes, food and drink, and the bandages, painkillers and antiseptic needed to treat the GSW. And at least they would be alone.

Danny glanced down the road in the direction of the station. The train must have arrived, as a number of people were walking up toward the parking lot. Elena was easy to spot—there were not many black faces in that part of Wales. But Danny waited, wanting to be certain that she was not being followed. He watched her walk to the café and go inside and then looked carefully at the other pedestrians. It seemed fine: no one hovered by the door, or stopped and waited a few meters further up the road. But still Danny waited. After a few minutes Elena came out with two mugs of tea and sat down on one of the wooden benches outside the café. Danny had one more check in both directions and then crossed the road to meet her.

He sat opposite her on the bench. "Journey OK?"

"Yeah, no problem."

"I'm glad you're here."

"Danny, I need to—"

"I could really do with this." Danny wrapped both hands around the closest mug, lifted it to his lips and took a sip. He grimaced. "No sugar."

"That's not yours."

"Oh, right. You given up sugar then?" He reached for the other mug.

"Danny, listen—" Elena didn't get any further. She looked to her left and then raised her eyes to the heavens. "Oh, no."

Danny turned and saw the man approaching, a man he remembered only too well.

"Hello, Danny. Nice to see you again, son."

"Dad, I told you to wait," said Elena, standing up. "I wanted to talk to Danny."

"I did wait, darling. But I'm desperate for that cup of tea. You two lovebirds take a little walk while I sit here."

Joey reached for the mug Danny had been holding a few seconds earlier and took a long swig. "Mmm, there's nothing like a proper British cup of tea."

The way Danny glared at Elena made words unnecessary. He gestured for her to follow him and they walked off, leaving Joey to his tea.

Danny was almost speechless with fury. Almost. "What the hell is he doing here? Does he know what's happened? I can't believe you brought him!"

"I didn't have a choice," snapped Elena. "And if you'll listen for a minute instead of shouting, I'll explain."

Danny tried to stay calm as she told him what had happened outside Foxcroft: ". . . and he's got no money, Danny, and he shouldn't be in the country. He's more of a danger running around on his own than if he's with us. If that woman finds him, she'll—"

"*Us?* What d'you mean *us?* You're not staying with us."

"I am, Danny. For tonight at least."

"Elena—"

"Where's your granddad?"

"Miles away. I had to leave him."

"And how are you planning on getting back?"

"I dunno. I could maybe get a taxi after we've bought all the stuff we need."

"We've got a car."

"What?"

"We hired it in London—it was quicker than getting the train, especially on a Sunday. It's in the parking lot."

Danny had been trying to figure out how he was going to explain to a taxi driver that he wanted to be dropped by the side of the road with a whole load of shopping. "Yes, but—"

"You need me, Danny. And my dad can be useful. We don't have to tell him what's going on."

Danny nodded. Nothing with Elena was ever simple.

"Let's go and buy what you need," she said. "Dad's all right for a while—I've given him some cash."

They walked off in the direction of the superstore.

Danny sighed. "My granddad will go mental."

31

"I seem to remember being in a situation like this once before, darling," said Joey, taking a drag on one of his favorite foul-smelling cigars and blowing the smoke out through the rental car's window toward the brooding mass of Pen y Fan.

Dark clouds were gathering over the mountain and the fir trees were swaying and rustling. The rising wind swept the first drops of rain and most of Joey's cigar smoke back into the car. Joey ignored it. "Last time, we went to meet Danny's dad; now it's his grandfather. Any more members of the family lurking out there in the mountains?"

"No," said Elena, staring into the trees and wondering why Danny was taking so long.

"Mmmm. And how is the vicar, anyway?"

Elena turned and stared at her dad. "Who?"

"You told me Danny's dad was a vicar, moving to a new parish or something. So who's his granddad—the bishop?"

Joey was feeling a whole lot better. Being needed was good for his battered ego, and his old swagger and confidence were returning by the minute. But however much his ego had suffered, his memory appeared to have survived intact. What he said was absolutely true. Elena had invented a spur-of-the-moment story about Danny's dad being a vicar when she'd bribed Joey into driving her to Norfolk six months earlier, just before Fergus's rescue. The man Joey had met was the journalist Eddie Moyes, who'd been dumbfounded when this stranger started calling him reverend.

"Actually, Dad, the man you met wasn't Danny's dad, and he wasn't a vicar."

"No? You don't say." Joey was starting to enjoy himself. "Listen, darling, you're a wonderful daughter and I'm real proud of you, but you shouldn't tell lies to your old dad. Haven't I taught you to always be honest and truthful?"

It was more than Elena could take. "Eddie's dead! And he was a good bloke! And don't you dare start talking to *me* about telling lies!"

Joey took another puff at his cigar and threw the stub out of the window. "I'm sorry, babe," he said softly. "Look, don't you think you ought to tell me exactly what's going on?"

"Probably. But I can't. We have to wait and see what Fergus says."

"And this Fergus, he's Danny's real granddad?"

"Yeah."

"Well, I reckon the boy should be ashamed of himself."

Elena stared at her dad. "Ashamed? Why?"

"Bringing an old man into this wild countryside and allowing him to fall and injure his leg. It's not right. He should be at home, watching the television, putting his feet up, taking it easy."

Elena smiled. "He's not that sort of granddad."

"No? So what sort of granddad is he then?"

"Well he's . . . he's fit and strong usually, and he's . . . Oh, I don't know, you'll see for yourself when you meet him."

"When," said Joey with a sigh. "What's keeping them?"

What was keeping them was that Danny was having to re-dress his grandfather's wounds, as well as trying to explain exactly why he'd turned up with reinforcements.

Fergus took the news a lot better than Danny had expected, partly because the loss of blood made him too weak to put up much of a protest. But he could also see the logic of having someone, even someone as unreliable as Joey, driving them back to London. It would be a lot less complicated than struggling with buses and trains.

Danny had managed to locate most of the items Fergus had told him to buy, and following his grandfather's instructions, he set about patching up the leg as well as he could.

He cut off Fergus's jeans by running a sharp pair of scissors up the outside of each leg and then peeling back the blood-soaked denim. Next he poured a whole bottle of mild antiseptic fluid all over the makeshift sweatshirt dressings still wrapped around the leg.

"Use another bottle," said Fergus, flinching as the liquid soaked through the material and onto the wound itself. "It'll moisten everything up, and stop any flesh scabbed onto the material from ripping when you pull it off."

Danny took a deep breath: that was the bit he wasn't looking forward to, but he knew it had to be done. Gently and slowly, with Fergus catching his breath and grunting in pain, Danny pulled back the pieces of sweatshirt to expose the wounds.

It looked bad: the round had passed through the thigh but had fortunately missed the bone, leaving entry and exit wounds on the front and side of the leg. The flesh was a dull red and small pus spots were forming around the edges of both wounds. Danny stared in fascination, moving his head closer to inspect the damage, like a surgeon preparing for an operation.

"What the hell are you doing?" hissed Fergus. "Get on with it, will you!"

"Sorry," said Danny, grabbing more of the antiseptic fluid and a roll of cotton wool. Tentatively he cleaned away the dried blood and grass and mud stuck to the skin. But it was hurting Fergus a lot, and Danny decided that talking might at least help take his grandfather's mind off the pain.

"Me and Elena have a plan."

"Oh yeah?" said Fergus, picking up on Danny's line of thought. "So tell me about it." At that precise moment he didn't care what Danny had to say—anything that distracted his brain from the gnawing agony would help.

"Joey gets us back to London, drops us off at a hotel or B and B— anywhere we can get you in without drawing too much attention to ourselves. Elena's gonna try to contact someone on the Deep Web, like she did before. Maybe some real hacker will have a program that can get us into the Northwood mainframe. And if there's proof there about you being a K, she downloads it onto her PC. Then we've got it. For good."

Beads of sweat were standing out on Fergus's brow. He let his head fall back so that the raindrops dripping from the firs could fall onto his face. And while the rain soothed his brow he focused on what Danny had said and attempted to concentrate on the bigger, fuller plan that had to be formed and fixed.

Danny worked slowly. His grandfather's biggest worry was that

without antibiotics to fight off infection, the wounds could go sep-
tic. Once Fergus was satisfied the flesh was clean, he talked Danny
through the process of placing gauze dressing over the damaged
areas and then evenly wrapping one-hundred-millimeter bandages
around the leg.

Finally he carefully pulled on the pair of loose-fitting tracksuit
bottoms that Danny had bought from the superstore, while Danny
changed into his own new clothes.

"I'll stitch the wound up when we've got more time," Fergus
said as Danny helped him to stand on his good leg. "Now let's go
meet our chauffeur."

He put one arm over Danny's shoulders so that most of his
weight was being taken by his grandson and then nodded that he
was ready to move. "It's a good plan, Danny," he breathed. "You've
done brilliant the last couple of days."

Danny said nothing as they edged slowly over the damp
ground. But he smiled; he wasn't used to being praised by
his grandfather.

Elena gasped as she saw them emerge from the trees. Even from
some way away she could see that Fergus looked awful. He was pale
and grimacing in pain as he hobbled toward the car. He seemed to
have aged ten years since the last time she had seen him. She threw
open the door and rushed over to help.

Joey was just behind her. "Take it easy, old-timer," he said, grabbing Fergus's other arm and pulling it over his own shoulder so
that he and Danny could take the injured man's full weight. "And
don't you worry, Grandpa, we'll soon have you out of here."

Despite the pain, Fergus turned his head and glared at Joey. "It's
Fergus," he growled. "Just get me in the car."

32

The rain was falling heavily and the windshield wipers were going at full speed as Joey headed east from Wales into England and toward London. And Joey was doing a lot of thinking.

His three passengers remained mostly silent for the first couple of hours, warding off their driver's clumsy attempts at questioning them.

They reached the motorway in darkness, with the rain bouncing off the vehicle, and at the first service area Joey pulled off the road to take a rest. He parked the car, switched off the engine and turned in his seat to face Fergus. "So tell me, *Fergus*," he said deliberately. "What exactly is going down here?"

Fergus was ready to draw Elena's father into his plan. "Nothing for you to worry about," he said deliberately, ensuring that Joey would want to know more. "Or get involved in."

Joey grinned. "But I *am* involved. And I know this for sure: you and Danny ain't been climbing no mountains, and whatever's wrong with your leg, it didn't happen tripping over no stone."

Danny and Elena waited for Fergus to speak, both of them wondering what he could say that would go even partway to satisfying Joey's curiosity.

"You're right," he said at last, looking directly at Joey. "It wasn't an accident. I've been shot."

Danny and Elena stared; the last thing either of them had expected to hear was the truth.

"I'm going to have to trust you, Joey," Fergus continued. "Can I do that?"

Elena couldn't believe what she was hearing. "Trust him? Of course you can't trust him. This is my dad you're talking to!"

Fergus managed a slight smile. He knew they were in big trouble: his wound was bad and there was no way he could just get out of the car and walk away when they reached London. They needed Joey's help, and while Fergus had no intention of taking Elena's totally untrustworthy and unreliable dad into his confidence, he wanted to give him the impression that he would.

A white van pulled into a parking space a few meters away and Fergus waited until the driver got out and ran through the rain toward the lights of the service area.

"You two go and get yourselves a cup of tea," he said to Danny and Elena. "I need to have a little chat with Joey."

For a moment Joey's eyes widened in alarm. "Wait a minute! You're not carrying a gun, are you?"

"You've got nothing to worry about, I'm completely unarmed." Fergus didn't bother mentioning the PE and detonators nestling in his jacket pockets. He turned to Danny. "Give us a while and bring me back some tea, plenty of sugar. And some food. And watch out for the CCTV."

Elena grabbed her laptop bag as she got out. "I'd better check my e-mail, see if there's anything from our friend. And I must call Jane to tell her I'm OK."

The rain was still falling heavily. Danny and Elena pulled down the baseball caps they were wearing low over their eyes and ran through the puddles toward the shop and fast-food area.

"He's not really gonna trust him, is he?" asked Elena as they reached the shelter of the buildings.

Danny laughed. "My granddad doesn't trust anyone. He must be planning to do some sort of deal."

Elena frowned. "Deals with my dad don't usually work out too well. Come on, I'm hungry."

They bought tea and sandwiches and a one-hour access card for the service area's hot zone and took them to a quiet corner. Elena made her call to Foxcroft and then checked her e-mail; there was a brief message:

Your friends are missing. Have they contacted you? Report.

"Don't reply," said Danny. "We'd better check with my grand-dad first."

"Take them some tea and sandwiches, and ask him what he wants me to do. But don't be long."

"Why?"

"Because I'm going into the Deep Web. Don't want to miss it, do you?"

Danny hurried away and Elena spoofed her ID, calling herself Gola, the name she had used on her previous journeys into the Deep Web.

She began hitting the websites she had used before to gain access to the Intelligence Service's internal computer system and George Fincham's personal e-mails. That time she had been helped by a hacker using the name Black Star, who was surfing the dark corners of the Deep Web.

Elena was good at hacking, but compared to the experts who dwelt down in the Deep Web she was still a novice, a script kiddie. She hit the site where hackers receive credits for their exploits, and where Black Star had first popped up on her screen.

Just like last time, Elena knew she would need a script written by an experienced hacker to get her past the firewalls protecting the Northwood mainframe. Just like real fire doors, firewalls are sometimes left open; if she could get through them, Northwood would be hers and she could go wherever she wanted.

Danny came back and sat down next to Elena. "My granddad says don't reply to the e-mail. How's it going?"

"Takes time, Danny," said Elena without looking away from the screen. "But at least I know the way now."

She bounced further down into the Deep Web, asking on the websites for any scripts that could help her. It was like being in an ever-expanding universe that seemed to stretch away into infinity.

The sandwiches were long finished and the half-drunk tea was stone cold when a pop-up suddenly appeared on the screen.

Hello again Gola. Remember me? I've been looking for you. You haven't been here in the darkness for quite a while. Wanna read what Black Star has for you? I can get you in there. Y or N?

Elena smiled. "This guy must live on the Deep Web."

"You sure it's Black Star?"

Elena pressed the Y key. "We're just about to find out."

I knew you would. Root access gonna be pretty hard to get, even I'll need help. Maybe Black Star and Gola can work together? It'll be the ultimate exploit. Y or N?

Soon they were reading Black Star's proposal. It said that Black Star would send two scripts to give root access. One script would run from Gola's laptop and would tunnel its way into the Northwood system.

That was the good news; the bad news was that the second script had to be burned onto a CD and then someone would have to put that CD into a computer inside Northwood.

Danny was staring at the screen. "How are we gonna get in there? It'll be guarded like the crown jewels. And if we do ever manage it, we know who that someone will be, don't we?"

Black Star explained that once Gola's laptop and the Northwood computers linked up, the two scripts, working together, would give root access. It was the only way, said Black Star, but if successful, it would have to be the biggest exploit of all time.

I won't see what you see, but hey, who cares!! You want the information, I just wanna be part of this exploit. Will you go for it Gola? Y or N?

Elena knew it was their only way of hacking into the mainframe. If even Black Star needed help, what chance would *they* have? She hit the Y key.

Ok! What an exploit! We're gonna be famous for this! You ready to download? Y or N?

By the time they got back to the car with more tea and sand-wiches for Fergus and Joey, the two men had made their deal.

Elena told Fergus the details of the Black Star plan as he sipped his tea. The whole concept of hacking and exploits was alien and strange to the SAS veteran and at first he was doubtful. "So what does Black Star get out of this?"

"The credit," said Elena. "It's what hackers live for; it's *all* they live for. It's our only chance."

Fergus nodded and finished the last of the tea. "Joey and me have come to an arrangement. He'll be helping us for a little while."

It was Elena's turn to be doubtful. "And what does Joey get out of it?"

Joey looked mortified. "Shame on you, daughter! You know full well your old dad would do anything to help out another human being in trouble."

"Yeah, right," said Elena, turning toward the steamed-up car window. She raised her hand and wiped away the condensation. The rain had stopped. "Isn't it time we got moving?"

They drove back toward London slowly, and at around mid-night Fergus told Joey to pull the car off the motorway and find a quiet place where they could grab a few hours' sleep. He was em-ploying ultracautious tactics: arriving on the outskirts of the city during the early hours and cruising the deserted streets would only invite trouble and the possible interest of a police patrol car.

But Fergus was in too much pain to sleep. Instead he tried to think of a way of getting Danny into Northwood while he listened to Joey's deep, rumbling snores and Elena's frequent complaints as she jabbed her dad in the ribs and told him to shut up.

Soon after first light they were on the road again. They stopped at another service area and Danny and Elena went inside for hot food and drinks. As they ate and sipped tea, Fergus outlined his plan for Northwood.

Even Joey listened intently. His eyes widened as he took in the details and he looked at Danny as Fergus finished speaking. "Rather you than me, son."

Elena was still in a bad mood from listening to hour after hour of her dad's snores. "I thought you said you'd do anything to help out someone in trouble."

"Yes, darling, but there's anything and *anything,* and this definitely comes in the *anything* category."

Fergus shifted his weight slightly in the backseat. His leg was throbbing constantly and the pain was increasing. He wanted to do the job himself, but he knew it was impossible. "It *is* dangerous, Danny. Are you sure you want to do it?"

There was no hesitation. "It's got to be done. Once this is over and we prove your innocence we can get you to hospital. So we'd better get on with it."

Fergus decided they should wait until after the early morning rush before driving into London, and they joined the A40 approaching west London at around ten.

The traffic was still surprisingly heavy and slow moving. They were close to Northolt when they spotted the reason why: a police roadblock.

"Trouble," said Joey as he slowed in the line of vehicles filing past the armed officers and parked blue Land Rovers.

Fergus stared out through the windscreen. "Don't panic. It's not for us. The police aren't involved in this."

Very few cars were actually being stopped; the volume of traffic was so heavy that it would have meant the whole of west London grinding to a standstill. Most vehicles were being allowed to drive slowly by, as officers peered inside to check out the occupants.

Joey was lucky, partly because the old red Ford Fiesta in front of them was directed to pull over. Three officers, all wearing flak jackets and carrying MP5 machine guns, approached the car, and without getting too close ordered the young driver, who was alone in the car, to step out.

Joey wound down his window and smiled broadly as he passed the lone police officer at the roadside.

"What's happening, officer?" he called as the car crawled slowly by.

The officer was already looking at the next vehicle. "Turn on your radio."

33

The third suicide bombing had taken place in Birmingham less than two hours earlier. This time only two people died, thanks largely to the heroic actions of a *Big Issue* seller out early in the New Street area.

It was a regular pitch: he usually recognized many of the office workers who passed by on their way to offices and shops in the re-developed part of the city. Most of them avoided buying one of his magazines; some adopting the no-eye-contact tactic, others using the old "Got one already, mate" line, when he knew perfectly well that they hadn't.

Monday morning was never a good time for sales; most people were too fed up at the prospect of returning to work after the week-end. But it was a bright, cloudless morning in the Midlands, and sunshine usually did help sales. So the *Big Issue* seller, who went by the name of Wilf, was out earlier than usual.

He spotted the smartly dressed teenager because he looked lost. And nervous. And because he was wearing an expensive-looking duffel coat over his shirt and tie, while most people were in much lighter spring clothes.

Wilf's only interest at first was in the possibility of a sale; he was skilled in sizing up potential buyers. He put this kid down as a well-off student, probably here for a job interview.

Slowly the young man moved up the incline toward Wilf, and at exactly the right moment—not too aggressive, in your face or confrontational—Wilf stepped toward him and smiled. *"Big Issue,* sir?"

The young man reacted as though Wilf was about to mug him. He almost jumped in the air, his eyes bulged in terror and he pulled his duffel coat closer around his body. It was almost as though Wilf had woken him from some sort of trance. He stood, frozen, for a moment and then shook his head vigorously and walked on.

Wilf watched him for a few seconds and then shrugged and turned away. "Have a nice day." He thought nothing more of it, but a couple of minutes later the teenager was back.

"Excuse me?"

Wilf knew it wasn't a sale; they never came back. The kid wanted directions. "Yes, mate?"

"Can you tell me how to get to the BBC? It's at a place called the Mailbox."

Wilf recognized the Newcastle accent instantly; his own girlfriend was from there. He pointed up the incline and gave easy directions to the new BBC center.

The teenager listened intently and then nodded.

"Got an interview, have you?" asked Wilf.

There was no reply; the young man simply walked away.

It was the mention of the BBC that did it. Wilf had watched the news, heard the stories of the smartly dressed young teenage bombers and their carefully selected, high-profile targets. He'd listened to the appeals from politicians and police officers for the public to remain vigilant and alert. And he was suddenly certain that beneath the young man's smart duffel coat there was a bomb strapped to his body.

"Bloody hell!"

The teenager was already about ten meters away and walking quickly. More people were moving up from New Street now and Wilf targeted the one he thought least likely to panic. He went up to a middle-aged man carrying a briefcase.

"Excuse me?"

"No, thanks."

"What?"

"I don't want a magazine. I bought one once before and found it completely unreadable."

"Look, I don't want to sell you a magazine, I need your help."

The man could see that this was no advanced-selling technique; the *Big Issue* seller really did look worried. "What is it?"

"Have you got a mobile?"

"Yes."

"Right. Well, don't panic when I tell you this. I think there's a kid heading toward the BBC at the Mailbox with a bomb strapped to his body."

The man's eyes widened, but Wilf continued before he could say anything in response. "Phone the police, say that *Big Issue* Wilf told you. They know me. Tell them the kid has got fair hair and he's wearing a black duffel coat. Oh, and he's from Newcastle."

The man nodded and reached into his pocket for his mobile phone as Wilf started to move away.

"Where are you going?" called the man as he began punching in numbers.

"I'm gonna see if I can stop him, talk him out of it. He's just a kid. Make the call. *Please!*"

The fair-haired teenager from Newcastle was nearing his destination when he heard a voice calling to him.

"Hey, mate?"

He stopped. In his right hand were a few twists of green garden twine. He tightened his grip slightly, slowly turned around and immediately recognized the *Big Issue* seller who had given him directions and was now standing a few meters away, smiling at him.

"What time's your interview?"

"My . . . my . . . ?"

"Got time for a coffee first?"

They were standing in a wide open space in front of the steps leading up to the Mailbox. The teenager looked confused: Wilf could see beads of sweat standing out on his forehead.

"I . . . I don't want any coffee."

He started to turn away, but Wilf called to him again. "Look, mate, I know you're in trouble and—"

"*Piss off!*" The teenager was shouting. "I'm *not* in trouble! Just leave me alone!"

Wilf raised his hands and held them open, with both palms facing forward. "It's cool, it's cool. It's just that I've had a few problems myself and I know what it's like."

"You know nothing! How could you know?"

Wilf was no professional negotiator; he just wanted to help a kid in trouble. Like he said, he'd had problems of his own. Drugs, and the increasing amount of theft required to fund the habit. But there had been people around to help him. He was clean now and going straight. His life was the best it had been for years.

But at that moment Wilf made the mistake that no professional would ever have made. Instead of keeping his distance, he moved closer, simply to reassure the teenager facing him; to show him that he was no enemy; to prove that they were on the same side.

He saw the teenager's right arm jerk upward and a momentary flash of brilliant light.

And then it was over. For them both. Forever.

Mark Davenport had left his home in Newcastle the previous evening after a fight with his parents. It was most unlike him; he was a quiet eighteen-year-old who rarely, if ever, argued with his mum and dad.

He liked living at home, so much so that when it came to choosing a university, he'd opted for Newcastle, despite receiving offers from more prestigious centers of learning. And it had seemed to be the right choice. His first year was going well, and even if Mark hadn't really made many new friends, he'd seemed happy enough. At first.

However, over the past few months Mark had gradually become more withdrawn, with little to say unless someone spoke to him. The situation at home became tense and his worried parents had finally confronted him with it the previous afternoon.

They reasoned to begin with, and when that got them nowhere, they argued, until Mark finally stormed off to his room. Half an hour later, dressed in a shirt and tie and his black duffel coat, he left the house and drove away in the secondhand white Nissan Micra his parents had given him as a surprise eighteenth birthday present.

At one o'clock in the morning Mark's anxious mother phoned the police to report her son missing; he had never before stayed out that late without phoning to say he was OK. The desk officer patiently took down Mark's description and was sensitive enough not to tell Mrs. Davenport that she was worrying unnecessarily. He was a dad himself; kids were a worry. He logged the details and asked Mrs. Davenport to call again when Mark turned up, as he felt sure he would.

But he never did. Less than an hour after the explosion in Birmingham, police had matched the facts from Newcastle with the city center CCTV footage and the details phoned in by the man Wilf had spoken to near New Street. Soon the identity of another bomber was confirmed and Mark's distraught parents were being comforted.

Police forces throughout the country swept into action even sooner, with new tactics, planned since the second bombing. Roadblocks were set up on major roads into cities, targeting young drivers traveling alone. Police were suddenly present on trains and buses, and outside schools and colleges. They were stopping, challenging and questioning teenagers, particularly those who were alone.

There was no longer any doubt: the bombings were part of an orchestrated campaign. But the vital question remained unanswered: who was doing the orchestrating?

34

It was like being in a white goods graveyard. Old fridges, freezers, washing machines and tumble dryers took up every available meter of space in the warehouse. They lined every wall and in some places were balanced precariously, one on top of another.

But they were silent; the only sound came from the hum of the fluorescent strip lighting dangling unevenly from the steel support girders stretching across the warehouse.

Joey and Danny helped Fergus through the maze of white and up the steel staircase bolted to one wall. On the first floor was one large room, with a filing cabinet, a desk, a couple of bentwood chairs and an old, threadbare sofa. A barred, grime-covered window looked out onto a small square made up of other industrial units. In the distance the massive steel arch and construction cranes of the new Wembley Stadium cut into the skyline.

Behind Park Royal Station and the lines of car showrooms and fast-food places that hug the A40 is a world of business parks, conveniently positioned to make use of the main road in and out of west London.

They were in the heart of one of the parks. They had pulled off the A40, passing a Renault showroom and a Parcel Force depot. The service road was potholed through constant use by heavy vehicles. Joey had known exactly where he was heading. He turned the rental car into the square and they stopped by the roll-down shutters outside a unit in one corner. They got inside quickly.

"Not exactly home from home," said Joey as he and Danny eased Fergus down onto the dusty sofa. "But I guess it will do."

Fergus nodded as Danny lifted his injured leg onto the sofa. "Just tell me again exactly how you sorted this, Joey?"

Joey sat on one of the bentwood chairs and took out a small cigar. "Like I said, this place was the legitimate side of my business partner Sonny's operation. I brought Elena here to meet him."

"Yeah, I remember him," said Elena as she unpacked some of the items she and Danny had bought while Joey had been arranging their new place of residence and Fergus lay in the back of the car fighting back the pain from the GSW. "And I didn't like him."

Joey lit the cigar and blew out a long stream of smoke. "No, well, we don't have to worry about good old Sonny. He'll be staying at Her Majesty's pleasure for some considerable time."

Danny was unrolling new sleeping bags from their plastic wrapping. "So how come we can use this place? And you've got the keys?"

Joey took another puff on his cigar. "While you were shopping, I went to see Sonny's wife, Joyce. She's a fine woman; I met Sonny through Joyce back in Nigeria a few years ago." He smiled and wistfully blew on the end of the smoldering cigar. "Yes, a fine woman. In fact, there was a time, a while back, when me and Joyce used to—"

"Dad!" said Elena, holding up her hands. "This comes under the heading of 'too much information.' We get the picture—you were good friends, right?"

"That's right—*real* good friends, honey. But Joyce has been struggling to keep the business going. So she's agreed that I can take over after I've spent a couple of days sorting out my own situation." He looked at Fergus. "That's where you come in."

Fergus nodded. "If we get out of this, I'll do what I can for you."

"I'm counting on you," said Joey as they watched Elena take her precious laptop from its bag.

"Can you get online here?" asked Fergus.

"All I need is a hot zone." She saw his puzzled look. "There'll be plenty around, I just have to find one I can access."

"Right. Well, I want to stitch my leg up while I've still got the strength, and you won't want to watch. You and Danny go and see if you've had any more messages from our friend in the Firm. If you have, you tell her exactly what I've told you and no more."

Joey threw his cigar butt onto the floor, trod on it and then stood up. "Think I'll take a ride. I'm not especially keen on watching medical operations either." He was already on his way to the stairs. "I'll go see Joyce—we've got a lot of catching up to do and—"

"Wait!" said Fergus. "I want you nearby; we'll need you to drive later. Go find those things I asked you to get me, but move the car first. Park it outside the square, across the road where we can see it. And keep it there from now on—we don't want to attract any unnecessary attention after dark."

"These things you want Joey to find?" said Danny. "I thought we'd bought everything you wanted."

"Just a few extras. For defense. Come on, let's move. Elena, what about your school?"

"School?"

"Won't they be worried if you don't turn up?"

Elena shrugged. "I'm sixth form. Sometimes I don't go."

Fergus nodded. "I need your computer bag, and Joey, leave me your lighter."

"My computer bag?"

Joey looked equally bewildered. "My lighter? Just what sort of operation is this?"

Fergus smiled. "They're for after the operation."

The 2lb-breaking-strain length of nylon fishing line was threaded through the small needle and was balanced on Fergus's good leg. He'd pushed his tracksuit bottoms down around his ankles and now slowly eased off the last of the bloodstained dressings from the GSW to expose the entry and exit wounds.

It didn't look good: the pus spots were getting bigger. One had burst and was oozing into the torn, scabby flesh. Fergus poured the last bottle of antiseptic liquid over the gaping wounds and doused the needle and fishing line as well. He held his breath and took the pain as the fluid attacked the exposed muscle. It wasn't going to help much—the wounds were far too infected—but the thought that it might at least stop them from getting any worse made Fergus feel a little better.

Fergus had performed this sort of emergency operation before, in the field; but never on himself. It was going to hurt, but there was no other option: the wounds had to be stitched up if they were ever going to heal. He could worry about fighting the infection when, and if, he managed to get some proper medical attention.

He took a deep breath, clenched his teeth and pushed the needle in at the start of the exit wound, tensing his muscles to absorb the pain. The needle penetrated the top layer of skin and slid through muscle until it pierced the raw flesh on the inside of the wound. It hurt like hell, but that was a good sign—at least the muscle hadn't gone dead and blood was still flowing around the wound.

With his left hand Fergus squeezed the two sides of the wound together, and pushed again until the needle broke through the skin on the other side. He took another breath and held it, pulled on the needle and watched as the fishing line slid through the two sides of the wound and slowly closed them together. He kept the needle held high in his right hand and his left continued to squeeze the wound together. The best way to combat the pain was to get on with it, so he moved the needle across and pushed it in again.

Gradually he stitched up the exit wound; nothing fancy or pretty, he just looped his way along, with the pain getting worse all the time. He couldn't allow himself to pass out. He could hear Danny and Elena speaking to each other downstairs. He focused on their voices, forcing himself to try to hear what they were saying, as he watched his skin being pulled up like a small volcano, with pus oozing from the top each time he tightened the fishing line.

Finally the exit wound was stitched. It would hold for now. The entry wound was smaller: stitching it would be easier. Fergus gritted his teeth and began again.

There were plenty of firms and individuals operating their own hot zones in the area, and as Elena had told Fergus, she just had to find one that didn't need a password for access.

She went onto her wifi network and a whole list of names appeared.

"A lot of people are lazy," she said, scrolling down to the first name. "Either they don't care who uses their hot zone and let anyone on, or they give it a name and then use the name as the password, so no one logging on has to remember anything different."

But Elena's confidence was dented slightly when she was unsuccessful with the first few names she tried. Each time she typed in a password matching the name, she was denied access.

"Maybe they're more security conscious around here," said Danny, wondering if they would have to go out and legitimately log onto a publicly accessible hot zone somewhere in the area.

"We'll find one," said Elena. "Just be patient."

Before she could try the next name on the list, the metal shutter at the front of the building opened noisily and Joey appeared clutching an empty five-liter paint can. He held it up. "You think this will do?"

"For what, Dad?"

Joey shrugged. "Don't ask me, darling. Fergus said he wanted a paint can. Found this one in the trash outside, and the nuts and bolts he wants." He shook the can and the rattling sound proved to Danny and Elena that it did indeed contain pieces of metal. "I'll leave this here while I go get some cardboard. There's plenty in one of the other Dumpsters, but I got no idea where I'll get the electric plug and lead he wants."

Danny and Elena exchanged a look. They had no idea what Joey was talking about but they could easily solve one problem for him.

"Dad, what is this place full of?"

Joey glanced around. "Fridges, darling. And freezers, and washing machines."

"And what have most of them got dangling from the back?"

Joey looked at the closest fridge and saw the length of electrical lead and the plug still attached to the machine. He smiled. "Darling, you're a genius."

He placed the paint can on the floor, stepped outside and rolled down the shutter, and with a shrug to Danny, Elena went back to her computer.

The next name on the list was OfficeHelp. Elena typed the name into the password box and suddenly she was online. She grinned at Danny. "Must be one of the firms around here. Very helpful they are too."

She logged onto her e-mail and the message they had half expected was waiting.

You do not reply. This is NOT GOOD. Where are they, and where are you? Report IMMEDIATELY!!!

"Think she's getting a little bit touchy," said Danny.
"Good."
Elena hit the reply box and typed in exactly what Fergus had told her to write:

All alive and safe.

She logged off just as the metal shutter rolled up again and Joey appeared holding a selection of cardboard in various shapes and sizes. He pushed down the shutter and picked up the empty paint can.

"Looks like Fergus wants to make something for *Blue Peter*," said Elena with a smile.

"Somehow I doubt it," said Danny quietly. "Let's go up."

As they climbed the stairs, the smell of burning wafted down toward them. Elena was first up, and as she glanced over at the sofa she saw Fergus blowing on one smoldering end of her laptop bag.

"That's my *bag*!" she shouted.

"Yeah, sorry, but you'll need this for the CTR. And I'll buy you a new one if we manage to get out of this alive."

Fergus had burned a small hole in one end of the laptop bag. He blew on the hole again, and when he was certain it was no longer smoldering, he dropped the bag on the floor.

He was looking pale and drawn and was obviously in agony from stitching up the GSW. But there was still much to be done before he could rest. "Sit down, all of you, and I'll run through the plan for the CTR."

Elena sat on one of the bentwood chairs and Joey claimed the other, placing the items rescued from the rubbish skips on the floor.

"Get everything?" asked Fergus.

"Everything you asked for."

Danny perched on one arm of the sofa and stared at his grandfather. His face was almost gray and there were dark shadows beneath both his eyes. "You all right?"

Fergus fended off the question with a shrug. "Now listen. You've got to realize that's it's not just the third party you have to worry about when you do the walk past at Northwood. This is a secure location and the security is good—the best—and with these bombings going on they'll be on a heightened state of alert. If they see *anything* suspicious, even outside the camp, they'll come and check it out."

They listened as Fergus gave them his orders for the CTR. He went through everything twice and then asked if there were any questions.

"Yeah, one," said Danny. "The CTR sounds fine, but what about me actually getting into Northwood? How do I do that?"

"I'm not sure yet," answered Fergus. "But I'm working on it, and I'll have a better idea when I see what you come up with after the CTR."

35

The red MoD sign pointed up the road and said simply: NORTHWOOD HEADQUARTERS. Joey pulled the rental car up to the curb, just past the junction.

They all knew the importance of third-party awareness from the moment the operation began, so as Danny clambered from the backseat and out onto the pavement he called a cheery "Thanks for the lift. Bye."

Joey and Elena came back with equally casual and natural farewells, and Danny closed the door and waved as the car continued on down the road. With his grandfather's warning of the tight security surrounding Northwood still fresh in his mind, Danny made a final check of the contents of Elena's computer bag, which hung from one shoulder, and then went back to the junction to begin the half-mile trek to the start of his CTR.

He walked along the leafy street dotted with large detached houses with long drives and signs bearing names like Chestnut House and The Paddocks. As he strode purposefully along, he reflected that there were a lot of "what if's" to consider, ranging from "What if I check the camcorder after the walk past and there's nothing on the screen?" to "What if Joey isn't there for the pickup?"

He would tackle those situations if they happened, but for now he had to be prepared for the "What if I'm stopped and asked what I'm doing?" scenario. He ran through his cover story. It should be good enough to satisfy the curiosity of any MoD policeman, and it was the truth, anyway; he was on his way to meet his friend Elena. The only problem would come if he were asked to reveal what was inside the computer bag. Then the game would be up.

The whole country was nervous since the third suicide bombing. Fergus had heard enough in radio reports to know that it was a complication they could have done without. He had insisted that Danny wear no jacket, just a sweatshirt, so that it was perfectly clear that there were no explosives strapped to his body, hidden beneath a bulky coat.

The houses gradually gave way to woodland and Danny knew from his briefing that he had almost reached his destination. He unzipped the computer bag, reached inside to power up the camcorder nestling at the bottom and then zipped up the bag again as he continued walking.

He reached a four-meter-high fence on the other side of the road. Beyond that, a gravel path followed its perimeter, stretching all the way around the Northwood complex. Soon afterward an MoD police car, two up, slowly cruised by. Danny glimpsed the MP5s strapped across the officers' chests as the one in the passenger seat gave him the once-over. But the vehicle didn't stop.

Danny made sure the small hole Fergus had burned in the slim laptop bag was facing toward the target to ensure that the camcorder filmed everything he could see. The camcorder had been the most expensive item on Danny and Elena's shopping list earlier in the day, but Fergus had told them that the video was essential as it would give him the vital information he needed to devise a way of getting Danny inside Northwood.

The bag fit was a simple device, but really effective because of the way a camera lens works. The camera was securely taped into position, with its lens hard up against the hole in the computer bag: this was smaller than the lens itself, but because a lens automatically brings the image into its center to project it into the camera, it could still function perfectly and yet be completely hidden. It meant that Danny would return with a complete, if jerky, record of his walk past Northwood.

Soon he was almost opposite the main gate. Behind the trees planted to hide as much of the camp as possible, Danny could just see the buildings. They were all close together, and a mix of old brown brick and modern glass and concrete. One was taller than the others—several stories high—and had flags flying from it.

Just past the gate, and inside the fence line, was a duck pond. Danny smiled; maybe they were trying to appear more people friendly. But his smile vanished as he saw the guardroom. Outside, on stag, were RAF personnel, dressed in DPM uniforms and armed with SA80 assault rifles. Concrete barriers were placed across the entrance to stop any car bomber from crashing into the camp.

Danny could see the tallest building with the flags a lot more clearly now. And so could the camcorder. He figured that the flags meant it was the hub of Northwood. But as a female guard stepped toward the gate, he suddenly realized he was paying a little too much attention to everything on the far side of the road. Danny could feel her eyes on him, and his heart began to pound: from somewhere behind the tree line dogs started barking and then an

RAF dog handler appeared by the gate with what had to be the world's biggest German shepherd.

The dog bared its fangs and snarled, and Danny wanted to run. He didn't, but he was thinking quickly. Ignoring this sudden interest in him by both guards and dog felt wrong, especially as Rover looked desperate to be free of his leash and earn his keep by demonstrating what a bad idea it was for anyone to get so close to his domain.

So Danny took a gamble, very glad that his grandfather was not around to see it. He looked across the road toward the dog and handler, and with a smile called, "Down, Rover—there's a good boy!"

The dog let out two loud, short, sharp barks and pulled harder on the leash. The handler said nothing but stared hard at Danny; so did the female guard who was standing close by. But they both seemed satisfied that Danny was just another cheeky kid with a big mouth, and as he walked on, they finally turned away.

Danny was feeling quite pleased with himself as he continued along the road. But then he realized that his little double act with Rover had been captured by the camcorder, which meant he was in for it when his grandfather saw the footage. He shrugged; tough—it was too late to worry about it now.

He was back in residential land, and five minutes later he saw Elena walking toward him, just as they had arranged. Joey had driven the long way around and dropped her off so that they could meet up. The plan was that they would now continue with the CTR together, while Joey did a recce of his own. He was due to meet them later in a supermarket parking lot close to the original drop-off point.

"Hello, stranger, haven't seen you for ages," said the smiling Elena as they met up. It was a good performance for anyone who just happened to be looking out from behind net curtains.

They crossed the road and walked back toward the camp for a little way before turning right into a street lined on both sides with houses. They were working their way around to the back of the camp to complete the CTR. Danny had decided it looked better if Elena joined him after the main part of the walk past. Walking together all the way around the camp might arouse suspicion. This way looked more natural. He had gone to meet a friend and now they were heading off in a different direction.

Elena linked her arm through his as they approached the fence line at the back of the camp. "Looks better this way," she said, pulling him a little closer.

Danny smiled. He wasn't complaining.

The Prime Minister was absent from the Commons chamber for the emergency debate on the teenager bombings. The home secretary led for the government, explaining that the PM was in discussion with the heads of the Security Services.

For once there was little party politicking. Opposition leaders were acutely aware that there was too much anxiety, fear and confusion running through the population for them to attempt any political points scoring. All sides were presenting a united front.

The Prime Minister was in the House, watching and listening to proceedings in the Commons on a monitor in a small office. Other screens in the room showed more disturbing pictures from around the country, as rampaging mobs were shown demonstrating outside mosques and taking out their anger and frustration on those they believed responsible.

An ITN reporter questioned one of the men demonstrating outside the mosque in Regent's Park, asking him why this was happening when two of the bombers had been white, and not even Muslims.

"Don't mean nothing," snarled the man angrily. "They were converts—must have been—we all know it's happening all the time. This is a Muslim thing, this is what they do. It's them all right."

Dudley was in the room with the Prime Minister. He remained calm and composed as the nation's leader turned from the screen and stared at him accusingly.

"Disturbing, Prime Minister, yes, but, however unpalatable, we continue to believe that allowing the people a focus for their anger is the correct course of action for now. The public has concluded that the bombings are the responsibility of Islamic fundamentalists and many of our friends in the media are helping us by perpetuating the myth."

On one screen, in the packed chamber the home secretary was appealing for calm; another showed the scenes outside the Regent's Park mosque, where bricks were being hurled at the building.

Dudley coughed just loudly enough to regain the Prime Minister's attention. "It is a regrettable situation, sir, of course, but ultimately it's retrievable. And it gives us the breathing space we need to pursue the real perpetrator, or perpetrators, without them becoming aware that we are closing in."

"And *are* you closing in?"

Dudley's shrug was noncommittal. "We learn more after each attack, sir."

"I want to be informed the minute you have any developments."

"Yes, Prime Minister."

The strange assortment of bits and pieces that Joey had rescued
from the Dumpster was sitting on the desk. Along with the PE and
detonator Fergus had carried with him since the attack on the
house in Spain, they were about to be turned into a lethal and dev-
astating PAD.

The industrial unit had to be defended. There was no escape
route, only a single way out through the front. If Fincham's team
discovered the LUP the only option would be to fight.

Fergus had already weighed up the positives, and as far as he
could see there were just two. Positive one was that there were single entrances to both the square and the building itself, which
made it reasonably defendable.

If an attack team *did* approach through the entrance to the
square it would be met with positive two—the PAD; there was no
way they would be expecting that. But it was a one-off, one-shot,
one-chance weapon—not what Fergus would have chosen if there
had been a choice.

His leg was throbbing like hell and had stiffened up so much
he could hardly move. But while he waited for his own motley
team to return from the walk past, he could at least do something useful.

He took the five-liter paint can and stood it on the floor. The
bottom of the improvised device was the business end of the
weapon, from where the damage would be done.

Outside in the square, Fergus could hear a forklift buzzing

around and voices shouting as a truck pulled in to make a delivery to one of the other units.

He ripped one of the pieces of cardboard into a long rectangle before twisting it into a cone shape that would fit into the paint can. It had to slide in so that the tip of the cone pointed toward the open end of the can and the bottom fitted as tightly as possible against the base.

As Fergus made a few minor adjustments to the cardboard he listened to the voices outside. A row was developing between the truck driver and the manager of the unit he was meant to be delivering to. "It's cat! Cat! I told them *dog*. I specifically said dog! If I'd wanted cat, I'd have said cat. It's cat next time."

"Look, mate, it's all the same to me. Cat, dog, I just deliver the stuff, I don't eat it!"

Fergus smiled as he turned over the cone and began to fill it with the nuts, bolts and other small items of scrap metal that Joey had found. He packed in as many pieces as he could, filling the cone to the brim, and then picked up the can with his free hand, turned it upside down and fitted it over the cone. When he turned it back the correct way, none of the scrap metal fell out and the cone fitted tightly against the bottom of the can.

Next Fergus gently rolled handfuls of the plastic explosive in his hands to warm it up, making it more pliable, and then started packing it around the cone, pushing it carefully down against the cardboard so that the nuts and bolts were held more firmly in position. Before long the cone was no longer visible and the can looked as if it were three-quarters full of PE.

Outside, the delivery driver's day was not getting any better as he spoke on his mobile phone. "Yeah, he wanted me to take it back!

I've spent three bleedin' hours crawling around the North Circular and he don't want the stuff. You speak to him—tell him I'll bring dog food next time."

The mobile phone conversation was a useful reminder to Fergus as he prepared for the dangerous part of the operation. Elena had left her mobile with him so that they could report back when the CTR was completed. He took the phone from his tracksuit pocket and switched it off.

There was a lot of electricity as well as plenty of mobiles around the unit, which made playing with a det extremely risky. Once the detonator wires were untwisted and free they could pick up radio waves from the environment and spark a detonation. There was only a small amount of explosive in the tiny aluminum tube, but it was enough to blow off both Fergus's hands.

He took the det from his inside pocket while at the same time he reached out for the ten meters of electrical wire that had been taped together from the leads Joey had cut from the backs of a few washing machines. One end still had a plug attached and the other had three bare wires. Fergus checked that the plug and lead were working by using an electrician's screwdriver they'd found among the few tools in the unit.

He pushed the plug into a socket, switched it on and then touched the bare wires with the screwdriver, keeping his thumb on the end. A small red bulb in the handle lit up, indicating that power was running through the leads.

As he worked on, he checked the screwdriver itself several times by simply placing a thumb on the screw head and a little finger on the small metal disk on top of the handle. The bulb lit up each time because there was enough electricity in the body to complete the circuit. He then pulled the plug from the socket and earthed the wires by scraping them against the bare water pipe running along the bottom of the wall.

Fergus was drawing on all his explosives expertise from his years with the Regiment. He knew all the tricks—and all the potential hazards—including the fact that wires can retain an electrical charge. He had no intention of attaching the det and losing his hands through stupidity or bad drills.

He slowly untwisted the two det wires and attached one to the live wire on the lead and one to the negative, leaving the earth to dangle free.

Everything was now prepared; all that remained to be done was to very gently push the detonator into the PE so that it was in the middle of the can, exactly above the tip of the cone beneath. The PAD was ready.

Fergus dragged himself to his feet, using the bars on the window for support, and looked down onto the square. Directly opposite, on the far side, was the parked delivery truck. The unit manager was now arguing with his pet food supplier on the mobile phone as both the truck and forklift drivers leaned against the vehicle and waited for the row to be settled.

The entrance to the square was at ten o'clock to the front of the unit, with units to either side of the gap leading to the road. This was the target area for the PAD; it would be aimed at the entrance so that it could take out any attackers as they entered the square.

The windows were covered with muck and grime, and helped hide Fergus from anyone outside as he jammed the can between the bars and positioned it so that it was pointing at the entrance, about thirty meters away.

Once it was secure, Fergus covered the can with some filthy old tea towels that looked like a serious health hazard, and then pulled across the one curtain remaining on the rail until the PAD was hidden from both directions. Fergus was working on the "out of sight, out of mind" principle. If it wasn't in view, it wouldn't be disturbed.

He tied the lead in a knot around one of the bars so that if it were accidentally kicked or pulled, it wouldn't disturb the PAD, taking it off aim or pulling out the det. Then he ran the lead along the bottom of the wall to a plug socket; every hobbling step was excruciatingly painful. He knew the socket had power; it was the one he had used to test the lead. But he checked again with the electrician's screwdriver. Check and Test. Check and Test. Fergus had often thought those three words would be a more appropriate SAS motto than the famous *Who Dares Wins*.

Everything was set. Fergus slipped the screwdriver into his pocket and left the plug lying on the floor. It would only be pushed into the socket in the event of an attack.

He leaned back against the wall, exhausted. Now that the PAD was completed it was safe to use Elena's mobile. He powered it up and ran through in his mind exactly what would happen should the PAD be fired. It was a simple and very basic device. Once the plug was in the wall and switched on, the power would surge down the wire and initiate the det, which in turn would detonate the PE. The entire process would take just a nanosecond.

Because of the way the PE was shaped around the cardboard cone, it would produce what is known as the "Munroe effect"; this meant that seventy percent of the energy produced by the explosion would surge forward, toward the entrance of the square. At the same time the explosion would be so powerful and hot, it would instantly melt the nuts and bolts inside the cone and shoot them forward as a mass of white-hot metal, with enough power to penetrate even an armored vehicle.

If the molten metal were to hit a car, the vehicle would be lifted off the ground and ripped apart like a paper bag. The intense heat would instantly detonate the fuel tank and turn the car, and anyone inside it, into a fireball before it even hit the ground again.

But that only accounted for seventy percent of the force. The remaining thirty percent would burst out in every direction, taking out the window and the front wall for starters.

Everyone inside the room would have to take cover, or they would be blown to pieces. Even then they might not survive the sheer force of the detonation. It would be a huge explosion, with shards of glass and shattered brickwork hurtling through the room, each piece potentially lethal. No one would come out of it completely unscathed, but Fergus knew it was a risk worth taking. They would be unable to defend themselves, and would be killed anyway if Fincham's team were allowed to gain entry into the unit. This way, they had a chance.

Fergus was breathing heavily: the effort of moving unaided had completely drained him. He heard the delivery truck's engine start up and the vehicle move away. The cat food was beginning its journey back around the North Circular.

As Fergus thought about crawling back to the relative comfort of the old sofa, he felt the mobile begin to vibrate in his pocket.

Wearily he pulled out the phone and read the text:

CU IN 20

Fergus smiled, relieved that they were safe. He would run them through the drill on what to do in the event of the PAD having to be initiated. He was used to snatching sleep when he could. On operations the rule was: whenever there's a lull in battle, get your head down because you never know when the chance will come again. He had twenty minutes, so he closed his eyes.

36

The shutters of the other units had been closed and locked and the final vehicles had driven away. It was dusk and Fergus wanted to keep the lights in their unit off at all times. There was enough spill from the security lighting in and around the industrial estate to provide them with sufficient illumination.

The others had listened silently while Fergus explained what they had to do in the event of the PAD being initiated. All the while, Joey's expression grew more alarmed and his eyes opened wider.

Before Fergus began, Joey and Danny had lugged three tall fridge-freezers and a heavy old cooker up the stairs. The PAD was fixed at the window at the left-hand corner of the room, so the old white goods had to provide protection on two sides. The cooker and one of the freezers were placed between the PAD and the socket that would be used to initiate the device. On the other exposed side they stood two freezers, and the old sofa was moved there too; together they would provide some protection if the device had to be detonated. That was the theory at least, but Fergus knew they would need luck as well as planning.

"And remember," he added as he finished his briefing, "whoever detonates the PAD needs to take a quick look around to see that everyone has taken cover, then keep your head down and your mouth open, hit the switch and hope for the best."

Joey's mouth was already open. It was gaping like a goldfish frozen in ice. "Mouth open?" he managed to gasp.

"With such a big explosion, so close, the pressure wave can break your jaw if you clench it tight. Better to keep it loose and your mouth open."

Joey's mouth dropped open again. He glanced nervously over at the disguised PAD and then edged his way cautiously across the room, putting as much distance as possible between himself and the device.

It was time to move on—Fergus knew that keeping everyone busy was the best way of countering their nervousness. "So let's look at the footage of the CTR."

They gathered around the camcorder to view Danny's filming of Northwood. The edges of the screen were a little blurred and the picture was jerky, but the target could be seen clearly and Fergus seemed pleased. "I've seen worse."

Danny smiled. Coming from his grandfather, that was a compliment. He kept the sound low—it consisted mainly of rustling noises as the bag moved and the roar of passing vehicles.

Fergus froze the picture at a point where it showed the fence line at the front of the camp. "See those signs on the fence? They're warning that dogs patrol the perimeter along that gravel pathway there—look, between the fence and the line of trees."

Danny knew all about the dogs; his mind went back to his encounter with Rover.

Fergus let the film run again and gave a running commentary

on what he was seeing. "That's a four-meter fence and it isn't barbed wire at the top. It's something far worse: razor wire. If you look above the fence there are CCTV cameras covering the whole length of the gravel path and the top of the fence. The minute anyone tries to get over the fence, the guards will be out with the dogs let loose in front of them."

The film showed the MoD police car passing and the MP5s on the two officers in the vehicle. Fergus was worried. "Those guys will shoot first if you get caught climbing over that fence, Danny."

The flags came into view above the tree line, masking most of the buildings. "Those flags, Danny—the building they're on is the one you have to get into. That's the one."

Danny's hunch had been correct; he had recognized the most important building. He kept his eyes on the camcorder as the jerky picture moved on. "There's a better view of it soon."

The pond and guardroom came into view, and then the female guard and the dog handler with his friend Rover. The sound of Danny's shout to the dog was just audible and he held his breath as he waited for his grandfather's bollocking.

"You can't resist it, can you? Always got something to say."

"I was using my initiative," said Danny quickly. "If I'd just kept my head down and hurried away they might have been suspicious."

Fergus let it go; there was too much more to worry about without dwelling on one mistake. And besides, he didn't want to put Danny down for using his initiative, even if it had been misplaced.

They got a better view of the main building, and as the film moved on, Fergus pointed out the few possible places for an attempt at getting over the fence. One was at a corner on the fence line, where two CCTV cameras were mounted back-to-back, with a gap of less than half a meter between them. "There's a blind spot in the camera coverage—you have to go for that. The best way is to lay a folded blanket on top of the razor wire and roll over it. The trouble is, it takes ages to pull it off. You'll have to leave it there and that could compromise you once you're inside."

The film stopped suddenly, and then picked up instantly at a point soon after Elena had joined Danny for the second part of the CTR at the rear of the complex.

"There," said Fergus, pointing at the tiny screen. "Those buildings are the married quarters and the gate in front of them is your way out, Danny. There's a simple tube handle that only works from the inside. Just stick your hand in and turn it. They never bother about people getting out; it's stopping them getting in they're interested in."

When the film ended, Joey took out one of his small cigars and lit it. The blue smoke curled around the room. "Looks bad to me—maybe impossible."

"No, not impossible," said Fergus, "but I'm not happy with it. We need more time to properly recce the camp and check out those possible climbing points. There's too many things that could go wrong right now."

Danny had been afraid that his grandfather might attempt to delay the operation. "But we don't have time. It's got to be tonight. Look at the state of you—you should be in hospital."

He was right, of course, but Fergus wasn't thinking of himself. "Time spent in recce is seldom wasted."

"I've heard all that a hundred times," snapped Danny. "All your clever SAS sayings don't mean a thing now. We *have* to go for it tonight. I know how bad that wound is—I've seen it."

There was a stunned silence. For the first time since Fergus had met his grandson he suddenly felt he was no longer in sole and total control of proceedings. He sighed. "But getting you over the fence is only part of it. What about phase two? That isn't sorted." He glared at Joey. "Or is it?"

Joey took a final puff on his cigar, dropped it onto the floor and ground it out with his foot. There was a growing collection of butts strewn across the room. "Everyone chill—you'll give yourself headaches. I can get you a pass."

While Danny and Elena had been doing the CTR of Northwood, Joey's recce had been in a pub, but he had been following Fergus's instructions. He blew out the last of the smoke and nodded. "You were right, there were RAF guys from the camp in there. Should be even busier tonight, and that's what I need: a crowded pub with everyone having a good time."

Phase two of the operation involved getting hold of a Northwood security pass for just a few minutes, so that a duplicate could be made. If Danny did, somehow, make it over the fence, there was no way that he could then just walk into a secure building, or even attempt to break in. He would need a security swipe pass for the main door and any internal doors he might encounter. And Fergus had devised a possible way of getting one.

Elena had bought a card swipe reader when purchasing the camcorder. And she'd learned how to use it by linking the reader up to her computer via a USB.

The gray plastic box was about ten centimeters long, with a groove running along it for swiping the card and reading the magnetic strip on the back. The readers are cheap to buy and are some-times used by unscrupulous restaurant waiters, who copy the card details from unsuspecting customers and then sell them on to crooks, who make duplicate cards.

All Elena had to do was swipe the security pass through the reader and the details would appear on her computer screen. Then she could burn those details onto the magnetic strip on the back of her own Halifax bank card.

Originally Fergus had intended to go into the pub close to Northwood Hill tube station, which he knew was popular with RAF personnel from the camp. His plan had been to get chatting with some of the RAF guys and then lift one of their passes, which would then go out to Elena, who would swipe the details. It was risky and dangerous, but no more so than every other element of the hastily conceived operation.

But once Fergus realized that he could no more fly to the moon than walk casually into the pub and stand chatting as he waited for exactly the right moment, he'd had no option but to turn to Joey for help once again. He didn't like it, but there was no other way, and he felt slightly better when Joey laughed and told him that it wouldn't be the first time he'd picked a pocket. Not by a long shot.

Now, after watching the camcorder footage and seeing for him-self the full dangers awaiting his grandson, Fergus was reassessing the whole plan. Ultimately the final decision on the go-ahead was still his. It all went completely against the maxim that he had fol-lowed since his first days in the Regiment: the famous seven Ps—Prior Planning and Preparation Prevents Piss Poor Performance. Piss Poor? This plan wasn't even *that* good. It was fucking crazy. But it was all they had, and as the nagging, constant pain seared through his leg, making him want to scream in agony, he knew that Danny was right. He wouldn't last long enough to come up with a Plan B. It was now or never.

Slowly Fergus nodded and then spoke quietly. "All right, we go tonight." He looked at Danny. "If Joey gets the pass."

Joey stood up, wandered over to the window and stared out through the bars. "Oh, I'll get you your pass. I've had more than enough of being cooped up in this place. I need to spend some time with the lovely Joyce."

37

It was raining. Just a light drizzle, but enough to dampen Danny's spirits as he leaned against the back wall of the pub and waited for Joey to complete the first part of the operation.

Danny felt uneasy. He could depend on his grandfather and Elena completely. He would trust either of them with his life. But Joey? Unpredictable, unreliable Joey? Even the thought of it was scary.

The strange thing was that ever since they'd driven away from the industrial unit, leaving Fergus to wait and worry alone, Joey had seemed to find a new confidence and sense of purpose. Maybe it was because he was at last doing something familiar; something he felt he was in control of. Or perhaps it was just that he was looking forward to getting the job done and re-establishing his relationship with Joyce.

Joey's greatest skill was his ability to mix and get on with people. He could be anyone and everyone's friend, and with the cash that Elena had provided in his pocket he intended to make a few very good friends tonight. So long as they were in the RAF.

He parked the car and told Danny and Elena that it might take a little while and that Danny should wait by the small frosted window at the back of the pub. On his recce earlier Joey had discovered that the window in the gents' toilet could be opened. He would lift the security card and then pass it out to Danny. Elena was sitting in the car on the far side of the car park with her laptop powered up, waiting to swipe the card and burn a copy.

Everything depended on Joey, and as Danny stood in the drizzle his thoughts drifted back to another apparently unreliable character he had depended on once before—Eddie Moyes.

Danny hadn't dreamed or even thought about Eddie in a while—too much had been happening—but as the raindrops dripped from the peak of his baseball cap, the nightmarish vision of his dream returned.

Eddie is running from the gunman and Danny is running toward him, trying to save him but knowing it's hopeless. Getting closer and closer as the pistol slowly rises in the gunman's hand.

He hears Eddie shout; always the same words: "Danny, help me! Please, help me!" He hears the words again. "Danny, help me! Please, help me!"

And then suddenly the words are different. This is new, strange, bewildering; even the sound of the voice has changed. It's still urgent, but not desperate, and the words are not shouted, but hissed in a loud whisper. "Hey, come on, Danny, help me out here. Danny!"

Danny shook his head to free himself from the confusion of the dream.

"Danny, what's wrong with you?"

It was then that Danny became aware of the hand dangling from the window just above his head. Joey was glaring out at him. "Come on, take this card. We ain't got all night."

The thoughts of bad dreams and Eddie Moyes were instantly thrust from Danny's mind. He reached up and grabbed the security pass. "Everything okay?"

"Sure, no problem. But I can't hang around in here too long—my friends back in the bar are waiting to hear another fascinating episode from my life story."

Danny went running across the car park to the rental car. He jumped inside and gave Elena the security pass. She swiped it through the reader and the details instantly appeared on her laptop screen.

87492820187633537840NH92826 2980

Elena pointed at the screen as she handed Danny a pen. "The last four figures—it's the pin number. You'll need it, so write it down."

As Danny wrote the numbers on his hand, Elena tapped the figures into her computer in preparation for burning the security pass details onto her own Halifax bank card. She needed to keep the security pass for a little longer just in case the burn didn't work and she had to start again.

Danny was impatient to get the pass back to Joey before its owner discovered it had been taken. "Come on, Elena, we haven't got all night."

Elena didn't reply or even look away from the screen. She continued with the job calmly and carefully, concentrating on getting it right the first time. Once she hit the burn icon, her own card would be gone forever as the details were erased. That was why she had withdrawn the maximum she could take out in any one day from an ATM on the way to the pub.

The card was ready to be burned. Elena hit the burn icon and swiped her Halifax card. Twice. Once to erase her details and then again to burn the security pass details.

She smiled. "It's done. Now go, go!"

Danny leaped from the car and ran back to the window, where Joey was still waiting. He snatched the security pass from Danny. "All done?"

"Yeah, we'll be waiting in the car. Quick as you can, eh?"

"Sure. But I got to pick my moment to get this pass back where it belongs. And I do believe it's my round."

Marcie Deveraux had spent a highly frustrating day and her evening had been little better. She hadn't appreciated receiving Elena's brief, insolent e-mail, and with Fincham becoming increasingly twitchy she knew that the time Dudley would allow her to complete her mission was running short.

She was in a foul mood as she walked toward her very exclusive members club for a late supper. The discreet ring tone of her Xda sounded and she answered the call with a bark, reminiscent of Fincham's telephone manner. "Yes?"

Curly was sitting in front of the monitor in the Pimlico safe house, and if he noticed Deveraux's impatient and aggressive tone, it didn't bother him in the slightest. He was about to make her day. "We've found the money! We know who the broker is! Fincham called him again to say he'd take whatever money he could. He's going over to get it, on the morning flight to Moscow, eight-thirty. We picked up everything: the conversation, the broker's number, the lot. It means you can get the money back, and I reckon I should be in line for a decent Christmas bonus."

Curly had every reason to feel proud of his achievement. After Fincham's first call to his mysterious broker, he had programmed the numbers Fincham had used to identify himself into the Firm's satellite ECHELON computer system. It meant that within seconds of Fincham giving his pass numbers again, they had been recognized and identified and Curly and Beanie were locked onto the call to Moscow.

"You've done well," said Deveraux. "I'll make sure it's mentioned."

"Yeah, he thought he'd be safe using another new pay-as-you-go mobile, but I got him. And that's not all—Fincham also called Northwood, said he needs to check some files. Maybe he wants to see if there's anything on the mainframe that could help trace him after he does a runner in the morning."

"What's he doing now?"

"Going though his papers, destroying stuff."

"That won't save him. Let me know when it looks as though he's ready to leave."

Deveraux ended the call and opened her e-mail, and as the club concierge opened the wide glass doors and she swept into the building, she reread Elena's old message.

All alive and safe.

Deveraux smiled. The end of the operation was close now; so close she couldn't stop herself from laughing. She had figured all along that Fergus Watts was the key to flushing out Fincham and recovering the money. And he was. In his panic to avoid exposure, Fincham had made a fatal error.

The money would easily be recovered now. Deveraux would phone Dudley and tell him that a team should be sent to Moscow to read the broker his horoscope and terrify him into handing over the cash. With full interest. Then, of course, he would meet with an unfortunate accident.

Fincham could be taken at any time before making his bolt for the airport, and Watts, Danny and Elena could be brought in. Deveraux would e-mail Elena that Watts was in the clear now that Fincham had implicated himself. All they had to do was turn themselves in, and after a debriefing they would be free to get on with their lives. Just as she had promised.

Deveraux had until 8:30 A.M. to catch up with Fincham. She would allow him to go into Northwood. She knew exactly what he was planning, but it would all be in vain. He wouldn't get to SECRET: ULTRA, where the real information on him was stored. Only the heads of the two intelligence services and the Prime Minister knew the access codes. Each had his own code; no one had all three.

Deveraux walked into the club's softly lit restaurant and dialed Dudley's number. She was looking forward to her meal.

It was almost closing time, and Danny and Elena were still waiting for Joey to emerge from the pub.

Danny was desperate to get on with the mission, but to do that Joey had to drive him up to the camp and Elena back to the industrial unit. After watching the camcorder footage again, Fergus had picked what appeared to be the two best places to climb over the fence. Danny had an old blanket resting on his knees, which he would sling over the razor wire.

Once over—*if* he got over—there were CCTV cameras, the guards and the dogs to worry about, before he even got near a computer and the information he would be searching for. In his pocket was a CD containing the script Elena had downloaded from Black Star, which had to be fed into a Northwood computer while Elena linked up with the mysterious Deep Web surfer so that they could make their combined assault on the mainframe.

But none of this could even begin until Joey came out of the pub.

"I told you he'd let us down in the end," said Elena, sensing Danny's growing anger. "He always does. I warned you."

"Maybe he got caught trying to put the swipe card back in the bloke's pocket."

"No way. If that had happened we'd have heard a police car by now, or he'd have been thrown out. He's in there getting drunk, or chatting up some woman."

The light drizzle had petered out, and Danny and Elena's conversation did likewise. They were both anxious to get on, but afraid of what the long night could bring. And sitting, waiting and wondering just made it worse.

The sound of shouted farewells and laughter drifted through the still night from the front of the pub and then Joey came strolling casually around the side of the building toward them.

Danny and Elena got out of the car to meet him and saw that he was smiling broadly.

"What the hell have you been doing?" said Elena angrily.

"Networking, darling," answered the beaming Joey. "That's what I do best."

"You stink of drink!"

"Well, of course I do. I made a lot of friends in there."

"I *knew* we could never depend on you!"

Joey took a single silver key from his pocket and held it out toward his daughter. "Depend on me? Sure you can depend on me, darling. You see that truck over there?"

Elena and Danny followed Joey's gaze to a silver Warrior truck, which had an aluminum top fitted to the cargo area at the back.

"What about it?"

"Well, that vehicle belongs to my new friend Richie. And he'll be heading back to the camp very soon, as he's tonight's driver." He turned to Danny. "You want a ride, Danny? I reckon it's a lot better than climbing that wire fence. You might cut yourself."

They rushed over to the Warrior and Joey quickly unlocked the top.

"How did you get the key?" asked Danny.

Joey shrugged. "Just took it off his keyring. Don't worry, he's got plenty more on there, and I don't imagine he'll be thinking of opening this up tonight, anyway. He's got three friends with him, and they'll all be riding up front in the cab. You got this all to yourself, Danny."

Elena was looking shamefaced. "Dad, I'm sorry."

"Forget it, honey. I never did like the idea of Danny climbing that fence, and when Richie started boasting about his wonderful Warrior, this seemed to be the answer." He held up the cover and looked at Danny. "Your carriage awaits, sir." He pointed to a small metal ring on the lock. "That's there so that anyone locked inside can get out. You just pull it and the top pops up. Now, you'd better hurry—they were finishing their drinks when I came out."

Danny was about to clamber into the truck when Elena grabbed his arm. As he turned back to her, she quickly kissed him on the cheek. "Take care. Please."

A few minutes later the Warrior, complete with four loud and laughing RAF men up front and one silent teenager hidden in the cargo area, pulled away from the pub's parking lot. Joey and Elena were sitting low in the front seats of their car, watching the truck as it moved quickly up the road.

Joey turned to Elena. "I thought you told me you two were just friends . . ."

38

It was cold in the back of the Warrior. And damp. But Danny found some small comfort in knowing that it would be just a short ride.

As the vehicle bumped over tarmac, he pulled his mobile phone from his pocket. Fergus still had Elena's phone and it was up to Danny to let his grandfather know about the change of plan. As always, Fergus insisted on being brought up to speed with every move.

Danny thought about sending a text, but the ride in the cargo hold was so bumpy there was no way he could hit the right buttons. So he found the number and Fergus answered instantly. "Yes."

"Change of plan. Found a new way into *the Obvious*. It's better. Others will explain when they get back."

He hung up. Danny had given his grandfather all the information he needed at that stage. He had carried out his orders, including his reference to "the Obvious," which was the name they had given to Northwood. To Northwood and more.

Just before Danny, Elena and Joey had left the unit, Fergus asked them, "So, where's Danny going tonight?"

All three stared at him, puzzled, before Elena said, "It's obvious, isn't it? He's going to Northwood."

"Exactly," replied Fergus. "But we don't want to advertise that to anyone, in any way. So if we talk about it, it's not Northwood, it's *the Obvious*. And that's a transferable phrase."

"A what?" said Joey.

"It can apply to anything we want it to. So if Danny gets the information we want, what has he got?"

Joey was looking more perplexed than ever, but Elena smiled. "Yeah, I see. It's *the Obvious*."

Fergus nodded. "Good."

Joey sighed and walked toward the stairs.

"You got it too, Joey?" called Fergus.

"Well, obviously," answered Joey without looking back.

There was just one other diner in the restaurant: an elderly military type, who was sitting with both hands cupped around a brandy glass.

As Deveraux toyed with her dessert, she couldn't help hearing the exchange between the waiter and the ancient club member as the bill was presented. "Was everything to your satisfaction, Colonel?"

"As always, Simon. Quiet in here tonight."

The waiter shrugged. "The bombings, Colonel."

The colonel grunted with disdain. "Despicable. They won't keep me away. If Hitler and his lot couldn't do it, I'm damned if a bunch of cowardly terrorists will!"

Deveraux went back to her food. She rarely ate a dessert. She was naturally lithe and athletic, supremely fit both physically and mentally, and she was determined to stay that way. Stodgy food could lead to a stodgy mind, and Deveraux's mind was always stiletto sharp.

But tonight she was celebrating the approaching end of a long and difficult mission with a very small portion of the chef's specialty, Belgian chocolate pudding. There wasn't much—five small forkfuls—and as she rested her fork on the side of the plate, the colonel's anger reminded her that the life she led meant there always would be another mission. Another battle to be won.

Deveraux's Xda, which sat on the pristine white tablecloth, began to vibrate; she had switched it to silent mode out of respect for her fellow diner, but even so she saw the colonel look up from his brandy glass and scowl.

She wiped her lips with the cotton napkin and spoke softly as she answered the call. "Yes?"

"You wanted to know when Fincham moved. He's just left his flat with one small suitcase. Next stop Northwood, I guess."

"Thank you."

She ended the call. The colonel was glaring at her; he was doubtless one of the "those newfangled telephone contraptions should be banned from the club" brigade. Deveraux smiled a conciliatory smile just as the waiter arrived at her table.

"Coffee, madam?"

"No, thank you, Simon. My bill, please."

The waiter nodded and melted noiselessly away.

Deveraux looked down at the last piece of chocolate pudding sitting invitingly on the plate and decided to leave it. There was much to do; her mind had instantly switched into operational mode.

39

The Warrior was parked up inside Northwood, close to the accommodation block. The driver and his three mates had left the vehicle fifteen minutes earlier, but Danny waited in the pitch dark of the cargo hold, just as Fergus would have done.

He ran through his grandfather's instructions on how to enter the building and reach his target area, the first underground level. It would not be staffed at this hour, unlike the two levels below that, which were manned around the clock—this was where military and covert operations throughout the world were controlled.

Danny held his breath with his mouth open. He was using methods he had learned from his grandfather over the previous six months, attempting to keep his own internal sounds from drowning out whatever noises were coming from outside the vehicle. He heard nothing: no footsteps or muttered conversation, not even a stifled sneeze or a distant cough.

He let his breath out slowly and then pulled the small metal ring on the tailgate. It popped open and he lifted the cover a few centimeters and looked out at the parked vehicles. They were damp from the earlier rain and glistened in the glare of the security lights. Everywhere was still and silent.

It was time to move. Danny lifted the cover fully, jumped out quickly and lowered the top. He remembered his grandfather's words: "Believe you are part of the camp. Once you're inside, move around as if you belong there, because the third party will naturally think you do. Security is designed to keep people outside the camp, so the deeper you are behind enemy lines, the easier it is to move around."

As well as the RAF guys, there were always civilian staff on the site, dressed in civilian clothes. Danny would be a lot younger than most there, but if he moved around with confidence rather than skulking in the darkness, he might just be taken for one of them. He had to believe he would.

The main building was about a hundred meters away. It was like a beacon in the night; every light appeared to be switched on. But that didn't mean it was crammed with people; the lights were on as a security measure.

A concrete path, with well-trimmed grass on either side, led to the building. Danny walked quickly and confidently along it, with his head down and his hands jammed into his jacket pockets. One was wrapped around Elena's Halifax card and the other held the CD.

As he neared the building, he found himself partially illuminated by car headlights from some way off to his right. He took a quick look and saw that a car was being held at the main gate. Danny could hear the engine running and he saw the driver stride purposefully into the guardroom.

The door of the main building was dead ahead. It was exactly as Fergus had described: a dark glass door, with more of the same overhead to protect the entrance from the elements. Danny's grip tightened on the Halifax card: his key to gaining access.

But then there was a moment of panic. People were approaching the door from the inside. It looked as though there were three of them. Danny felt his heart thudding. He had to carry on. If he turned and hurried away he would arouse not only their suspicions, but also those of anyone in the guardroom who might be looking in his direction. He had to believe. He had to believe.

He pulled out the card and swiped it through the reader on the wall beside the door. The door buzzed, and as Danny pulled it open he saw the three figures, all clad in DPM camouflage uniform, just a couple of meters away. There were two women and a man, and they were chatting about the week's leave one of them had just enjoyed.

Danny held the door open, his head tilted downward. As the three passed through, he concentrated on keeping his voice low as he muttered, "Evening."

One of the women answered, "Hello," and the others just nodded as they continued on toward the accommodation blocks.

Without turning to watch them go, Danny stepped through the door and allowed it to lock behind him. He had to keep moving and make it appear as though he used the door every day and knew exactly where he was going. Ahead was a long, narrow corridor with office doors on either side. The gentle hum of the air conditioners and the squeak of his own sneakers on the highly polished floor tiles was all Danny could hear as he ventured onward. That, and his pounding heart.

George Fincham was going through security clearance in the guardroom. Outside, his car engine was still running and two RAF guards were checking beneath the vehicle with flashlights.

The duty sergeant was showing Fincham all the respect he was due: after all, his ID card revealed him to be a high-ranking IB in the Intelligence Service. But correct procedure still had to be followed. "Now, sir, if you would place your right hand on the glass plate and look into the two eyepieces above?"

Fincham knew the drill. For positive identification his hand-print had to be checked along with his irises, but it all took time. Valuable time. "Just get on with it, man," he said, lowering his eyes toward the two lenses, which looked as though they should be part of a pair of binoculars.

"Won't take a minute, sir," said the sergeant as he forced a smile and pressed the buttons to set the machine in motion.

As Fincham looked into the lenses, he placed his right hand on the length of glass. A strip of light ran underneath, copying his handprint. At the same time lasers were focusing on his eyes, checking the unique pattern of his irises.

The sergeant was satisfied. "Thank you, sir." He handed Fincham a pass—a plastic card hanging from a white nylon strap with a large black *V,* for visitor, emblazoned in the center.

Fincham didn't even nod a thank-you as he turned away and went back to his car to drive to the parking area.

The sergeant and another guard, whose duty it would be to escort Fincham into the main building, watched him go. "What a happy chappie," said the guard as he adjusted his cap and stepped out into the night. "I get all the good jobs."

Danny took the stairway next to the elevator. So far it had felt as though the building was deserted. It wasn't. The place was like a warren. Many people were working on the levels below. Others might well be on the underground level that Danny was about to enter. CCTV cameras were fixed to the walls above the NO SMOKING signs. Someone somewhere could see what was going on. Danny had to believe he belonged there. It had worked so far.

He slid on a pair of plastic gloves, the type available to drivers at filling stations for protecting their hands from fuel. In Danny's case they were to keep his fingerprints off the keyboard once he got onto a computer. *If* he got onto a computer. He pushed through a fire door and stepped into the corridor of floor –1. He turned to the right, just as Fergus had instructed, and kept walking.

The layout was the same as on the ground floor. Danny was heading for room -1/44, the Stand By Room, which was reserved for use by visitors when they were working in the building. Fergus had been in the room many times when at Northwood for briefings.

Most of the office doors were closed, but as Danny walked along the corridor he saw that one up ahead was ajar. He heard a single voice speaking: someone was talking on the telephone. It was the duty officer. Danny didn't see him, but as he passed the room, -1/37, he heard the words, "Of course it's not. Who'd be using it at this time of night?"

Danny reached room -1/44: the sign on the door said STAND BY ROOM, and the door was unlocked, just as Fergus had told him it would be. He quickly went inside and closed the door. The room was in darkness apart from a soft glow of light emanating from the floor on the far side. The light silhouetted a desk with a PC sitting on top. Exactly what Danny needed.

He carefully moved over to the light and looked down at a long rectangular piece of plate glass, set into the floor where it met the wall.

Danny's eyes widened; he was staring down into the control and command center itself. It was one huge area, like an aircraft hangar. Massive screens covered the walls. Officers from all three services huddled around computers as maps and live video feeds from Iraq and Afghanistan filled the screens.

He wanted to stay there watching all night. But there was a job to be done. He turned away, powered up the PC and took the CD from his pocket.

The lift stopped at level -1 and the door glided open. George Fincham stepped out and strode into the corridor, with the escort struggling to keep up.

Further down the corridor the duty officer emerged from his room to meet the visitor. "The Stand By Room is ready, sir. It's just along here."

Fincham said nothing, just kept walking, and the duty officer fell in with his hasty step, the escort still trailing behind. When they reached room -1/44 the duty officer stopped, grabbed the door handle and began to open the door. "The Stand By Room, sir."

Fincham stopped walking and glared. "I'm not here for the Stand By Room. I'm going to the Depository."

The duty officer, a young flight lieutenant, exchanged an anxious look with the escort. The Depository was the most secure area in the building, where secret documents could be accessed and read. Even the walls were lined with lead so that radiation from the computer's screen could not be detected by someone out in the corridor with an electronic decoding reader.

The duty officer was well aware of his responsibilities. "But . . . but, sir? Do you have the correct clearance to access the Depository?"

Fincham had been expecting this and he was prepared. He was staking everything on this ultimate gamble. He pulled out his Intelligence Service ID card and thrust it toward the officer. "How dare you question me! Do you know who I am? Take me there now, or do I have to wake up your commanding officer and let you explain why his idiot of a junior officer is slowing down a time-critical operation? We are fighting a war!"

The standoff lasted for long seconds as the two men stared each other down and the escort watched. Then the duty officer buckled. "I'm sorry, sir. Of course not, sir."

40

Danny was still beneath the desk. He had dived down when he heard the footsteps stop and saw the door begin to open. He had listened to the argument, too panic-stricken to realize that the raised voice was one he had heard before, many months ago.

The operation had already begun when the interruption came. Danny had inserted the CD into the PC and was on his mobile, with Fergus at the other end. He had been ready to start the script. And then all hell seemed to break loose and he dived for cover. When the bust-up finally ended, the door was pulled shut and footsteps echoed away down the corridor.

Now it was quiet again and Danny still had the mobile clamped to his ear. "All clear." He clambered cautiously from under the desk and went back to the PC. The CD was gently humming in the drive and the PC was online. All that was needed now was to activate Black Star's script, which was on screen.

Wow! I didn't think you'd make it this far! So you wanna use my script? Y or N?

Danny's finger hovered over the Y key as he spoke softly into the mobile. "I'm ready to go. You ready?"

In the gloom of the industrial unit, with only the spill from outside security lights for illumination, Fergus and Elena were alone. Joey had been dispatched to wait for Danny at the prearranged meeting place outside Northwood. Elena's laptop was on her knees, her script was on the hard drive and she was connected to the hot zone, ready to go. Her screen also had a message from Black Star attached to the script.

Remember: The scripts must be run at the same time! Good to go? Y or N?

"Are you ready?" asked Fergus.

Elena held her finger over the Y key and nodded.

"Good," said Fergus. They had rehearsed the countdown. "OK, both of you. Stand by. Stand by. Go!"

Danny and Elena hit their Y keys at precisely the same moment.

Fergus and Elena watched as a matrix of numbers and letters swarmed across the laptop screen, constantly changing as a cacophony of telephone key tones burst from the speakers. Elena's script was trying to connect with Danny's.

The letters and numbers switched and changed faster than the eye could follow and the key noise grew until it sounded like one constant tone. They watched and waited.

And then everything stopped and the computer went silent.

Fergus looked at Elena and she shook her head. "I don't know. I've never done this before."

The seconds passed agonizingly slowly and still nothing happened.

"Black Star said it would work," breathed Elena. "That we could go anywhere we—"

Before she could finish, the laptop screen burst into life as pop-ups suddenly appeared on the screen as they passed into four different levels of security:

Restricted

Confidential

Secret

TOP SECRET: UK EYES ONLY

Elena laughed out loud; she couldn't stop herself. "We're in! We own the mainframe. We can go anywhere we want."

"Sshhh, keep it down," hissed Fergus. He spoke quietly into the mobile. "You got us there, Danny. You did it."

Danny could see that for himself as he read the four levels of security on his own screen. There was nothing more he could do now but watch and wait. Everything depended on Elena.

Another pop-up appeared on her screen, asking which operation or name was required. Elena typed in "Fergus Watts" and within seconds there were three F. Wattses on the screen, but only one with a regimental number.

"That's me, Elena. Let's find out what they've got on me."

Elena was amazed at what appeared on the screen. Details of Fergus's entire life, everything from his school history to hospital records and military career, were listed. There was even information on a conviction for speeding more than twenty years earlier.

But Fergus was unimpressed. "This is useless, it proves nothing about me being a K."

Elena looked up from the computer. "I could delete all this. You wouldn't exist. I could give you a new name, new social security number, new driving license, a whole new life. You could even claim unemployment."

"But in my head I'd always be on the run," said Fergus as he stared at a lifetime on the screen. "And Fincham won't give up until I'm dead, whatever I'm going by. The only place we'll find anything about me being a K or operating in Colombia is in Secret Ultra."

"Secret who?"

"It's the only place left that's worth checking, and getting to that is probably impossible."

"Maybe not for Black Star."

Elena went back to the Deep Web. Black Star was there. Waiting. Lurking. Eager for information on the progress of the ultimate exploit.

Elena punched in her request. Could Black Star help? Could Black Star get them to Secret Ultra?

She got an immediate reply:

Nothing you like so far?? You wanna go deeper? Chill, Gola, you want it you can have it. But this time you gotta give me a few minutes . . .

In the Depository at Northwood George Fincham was looking at his own life history as it rolled out on a screen. His national security and passport number, DNA, handprint and iris identification details, and medical, dental and university degree records.

Fincham was deleting them all, erasing every aspect of his life held on any mainframe, anywhere. Soon George Fincham would not exist. Everything from his bank accounts to his gas bills would be gone. George Fincham would have disappeared and George Davies would be flying to Moscow on the 8:30 from Heathrow.

Outside, in the corridor, the escort waited, having been told by Fincham before he closed and locked the door that he was not, under any circumstances, to be disturbed.

Fincham worked quickly but methodically. Soon there was only one place left to go; the one place no one would ever have known he was able to go—SECRET: ULTRA.

This was the reason why Fincham had demanded to be admitted to the Depository. There were only three places where access to SECRET: ULTRA could be gained: the offices of the heads of the Intelligence and Security Services, and the room Fincham was in now.

But Fincham did not need the three code holders, each with their separate codes, to be present. He took a USB memory clip from his jacket pocket and plugged it into the PC.

The screen went black for a second before a box popped up asking for codes A, B and C. Slowly three sets of numbers and letters began to appear next to the three corresponding letters.

Fincham smiled at his own brilliance and ingenuity. It was all down to the second Gulf War. Twice during the conflict he had been present as all three code holders entered their separate codes in the office at Vauxhall Cross to access the latest intelligence on Saddam Hussein.

The codes were long and complex. There was no fear among those present that anyone could memorize all three, not at the speed at which they were entered and for the brief time they were individually on screen. But George Fincham could. He was blessed with a photographic memory, and each time his eyes had flicked onto the screen like a clicking camera shutter, capturing the codes, which were then logged away in the photographic darkroom of Fincham's mind.

Later he had downloaded the codes onto the clip. As a backup. To ensure that they were never lost. Even by him.

The screen informed Fincham he now had access to SECRET: ULTRA. Fincham had no idea if there was anything relating to him in the files, but he had to know. Everything had to be deleted if he was to disappear completely.

He keyed in his name and Intelligence Service number and hit enter.

George Fincham *was* brilliant. But so was Black Star. There was a reference to Fincham in SECRET: ULTRA. It linked him to the one name to which he seemed destined to be linked forever: Fergus Watts.

And as Fincham read the file, Fergus and Elena were also reading it at the unit, and so was Danny, just a few meters away down the corridor in the Stand By Room.

41

In the warehouse, in the Stand By Room and in the Depository, four pairs of eyes read every word of the Sit Rep on Fergus and Danny.

For Fergus there was the first feeling of hope. At last. But it was guarded hope. "This is it. It's what we want."

"It's just like she told us," said Elena.

For Fincham there was an overwhelming feeling of horror. Primary target. It was him. His name was not mentioned as an added security measure. It didn't need to be. For those who needed to know, it was obvious.

"There's more," said Fergus to Elena. "Go on to the second page."

Elena scrolled through to the second page. Danny was doing the same thing. And so was Fincham.

SIT REP

MISSION: THIS IS IN THREE PARTS:

1. To locate and recover money (now estimated at around £15m). PRIMARY TARGET was paid by FARC while assisting them in trafficking cocaine into the UK.

2. On recovery of money, but before if recovery proves impossible, PRIMARY TARGET to be eliminated to avoid public revelation of treachery and corruption within SIS and subsequent embarrassment to SIS and government.

3. To "clean house." All those aware of PRIMARY TARGET's activities also to be eliminated for same reasons. This includes, but may not be restricted to, Fergus Watts, Danny Watts and Elena Omolodon. Before Fergus Watts is eliminated, every effort will be made to discover any other person or persons still living who are aware of PRIMARY TARGET's activities or of Watts's activities as a Deniable Operator ("K"). They too will be eliminated.

THIS DOCUMENT IS SUBJECT TO UPDATE.

M. Deveraux
M. Deveraux

All the final pieces fell into place; the picture became clear. For everyone.

It was what Fergus had feared all along, but all hope was not lost. His mind was working quickly. "Download it, Elena. Don't lose it."

Danny's voice came over the mobile phone that Fergus still had at his ear. "You're seeing it too, then? What they really want to do?"

"Yeah. Elena's downloading it."

"I heard. So do I come out?"

"Yes, but stay focused. Forget what you've just read for now, and concentrate on what you have to do. Don't get caught now, Danny."

Danny hung up, but before he could move he heard footsteps in the corridor. He dived back under the table.

The duty officer had returned to the Depository, where the escort was still waiting outside the locked door. "Is he still in there?"

"Yes, sir. I dunno what he's up to, but I haven't heard a thing."

There was no way that Danny could move until the two men and their visitor had cleared the area. Cautiously, he crawled out and went back to the PC; before leaving he had to remove the CD and close it down.

As he looked at the screen, the SECRET: ULTRA page suddenly disappeared and the screen went blank.

Danny stared and felt a surge of panic. If his computer had lost the page, then surely Elena's had too. But had she had time to download it?

As he stared at the screen, he heard another door open and then slam. He dived under the desk again. This was starting to feel like home.

Fincham had unlocked the Depository door and pulled it hard behind him as he walked out. "I'm leaving," he said to the startled duty officer and the escort. He took the visitor's card from around his neck and thrust it into the guard's hands.

He didn't wait for the lift but took the stairs up to the ground floor, with his escort scrambling behind.

"Go to the guardroom and tell the sergeant I'm leaving," said Fincham as he reached the ground floor. "I will not be stopping at the guardroom to check out. Get the main gate opened, man. Now!" He hurried away toward the exit, trying to control his fury. He had deleted the SECRET: ULTRA file—the evidence was gone—but inside he was raging. Fuming.

Marcie Deveraux! His own protégée. He had trusted her. Encouraged her. Nurtured her career. And all the while she had been plotting and operating to cause his downfall. But he was safe now. When he had calmed down, he would have the last laugh.

He cleared the main building and took a deep breath. In a few hours' time he would be on a plane to Moscow and this nightmare would be behind him.

42

As Joey parked the car across the road from the unit, Danny sent a text to Elena's phone saying they were coming in. It had been easy to get out of Northwood. Danny had walked to the back gate, fed his arm into the tube and pressed the button at the end. The gate opened with an electronic buzz and he walked into the married quarters, then out onto the road where Joey was waiting.

Danny hurried out of the car and across the square toward the unit's roll-down shutter while Joey made his more casual approach.

"Come on," urged Danny as Joey started to unlock the shutter door.

"You go on," said Joey as he slid the key into the lock. "I got something to do."

"Do? What d'you mean? We have to get inside!"

"Look, Danny, I been sitting there hours waiting for you. I couldn't move in case you came out. I got you back, I've done everything Fergus asked of me. Now I need a smoke."

"Then smoke here! We don't care!"

"I can't! I gave the last of my cigars away in the pub. I'm desperate, Danny. There's an all-night garage down the road."

"But my granddad—"

"Just tell him I'll be back before he even knows I've gone." He pushed open the shutter door. "Go on, I'll be fine."

Danny hesitated for a moment but then went in; if Joey wanted to kill himself with cigars that was up to him. He pushed the door shut and took the metal staircase three rungs at a time, shouting out before he reached the top, "Did you get it? Did you download it? I saw it deleted!"

Fergus and Elena were sitting at the laptop. "Yeah, I got it," said Elena. "Every word."

Danny let out a huge sigh of relief. He'd been almost hyperventilating with anxiety on the way back from Northwood, especially after there had been no response to his text saying that he was out of the camp and in the car. He didn't call for confirmation, partly because he thought Elena might have been struggling to download the information and a ringing phone at the wrong moment could have shattered her concentration, and partly because he couldn't bear the thought that all their work that night might have been in vain.

He slumped down onto the sofa, exhausted but elated. His grandfather was looking pale and drawn but he had just enough strength to manage a weak smile. "You did well . . . brilliant."

"But what it said, about us being—"

"Eliminated," said Elena.

Danny nodded.

"At least we know their true intentions now, and it's what I always suspected. But thanks to you two we've got a better chance of getting out of this than before." Fergus turned to Elena. "I need you to burn three copies of that file onto CD. Can you do that?"

"No problem."

"And then—" Fergus stopped and looked toward the stairs. "Where's Joey?"

"Oh, yeah," said Danny, remembering. "He's gone for some cigars. Said he was desperate."

"Bloody fool!" said Fergus angrily. "He should be here!"

Elena was already starting to burn the CDs. "He'll be all right. He'll be back soon, and at least we won't have to listen to him moaning."

Joey bought himself two packets of cigars at the petrol station. He slid his cash through the narrow gap beneath the toughened glass and metal-grilled window and waited in anticipation as the sales assistant reached for the cigars and pushed them through the gap, along with his change.

"Thanks, man," said Joey, smiling in anticipation of his long-awaited smoke.

The sales assistant said nothing. He turned away and went back to staring at the TV screen mounted on the wall above his till.

Joey wasn't bothered. "And a very good night to you too," he muttered as he ambled back to the car, unwrapping one of the cigar packets as he went.

He got into the car, pulled out a cigar and stuck it into his mouth. Having it there, unlit, was almost as good as smoking it—for a while, at least. He started up the car and drove away from the garage forecourt.

Then he heard the siren. He looked into the rearview mirror and saw the flashing blue light.

"Oh, shit."

The police car's headlights flashed a couple of times but Joey kept going: he wasn't going to stop unless he had to. Seconds later the police car came cruising by, and the officer in the passenger seat indicated for Joey to pull over.

Joey drew the car to the curb. This was not good; Fergus would not be happy.

The police vehicle stopped directly ahead and the officer in the passenger seat got out and walked back to Joey, who wound down his window and smiled, with the unlit cigar still in his mouth.

"Evening, officer. Lovely night."

"Very nice, sir. But did you know that one of your taillights is out?"

Joey cursed to himself. A dud light—they'd stopped him for nothing more than a dud light. He took the unlit cigar from his mouth. "I'm afraid I didn't. I'm extremely sorry, officer, I'll make sure I replace it first thing in the morning."

But the police officer wasn't finished. "Your car, is it, sir?"

"As a matter of fact it isn't. It's a hired vehicle."

"Can I see your driving license, please?"

"Why, sure, officer."

Joey began rummaging through his jacket pockets, all the while smiling a broad smile. It was then that the officer caught the strong smell of alcohol.

"Have you been drinking, sir?"

"Drinking?"

"Alcohol, sir. Have you been drinking alcohol?"

Joey's face registered the panic he was beginning to feel. "Well, no. I . . . I wouldn't say *drinking*. I just—"

"Would you step out of the car, please, sir?"

Joey sighed, slowly opened the door and got out. "It was only one. Just a pint—hours ago."

The police officer nodded and Joey held up the cigar, still gripped between two fingers. "Do you mind if I smoke this?"

"I'm afraid I do, sir. I'd like you to blow into this, please."

Fincham had calmed down. He was more his normal, cold, calculating self as he checked out his disguise in the disabled toilets at the service station on the M4, near Heathrow Airport. Gone was the smart suit, MCC tie and polished shoes. He was now wearing baggy cords, a button-up cardigan and sandals with socks.

Rolled out on the toilet seat was his makeup bag, along with cotton wool wipes. He had been busy and was putting the final touches to his disguise, comparing the Mr. Davies in his new passport photograph to the one he was looking at in the mirror.

Fincham was very pleased with the results. The trimmed beard stuck on his face lessened the need for more makeup. All Intelligence Service operators were instructed by professional makeup artists in the art of disguise, learning how to change the shape and size of their faces. Fincham had long ago mastered the art, and was a deft practitioner.

He touched up some of the darker makeup on both sides of his nose, the shading making it appear longer than it actually was. It would confuse the facial recognition cameras that scour airport terminals for known terrorists and criminals.

Once he had finished he put on a pair of plain lens glasses and the Mr. Davies look was complete. He appeared more like a bumbling university professor than an Intelligence Service IB.

Fincham rolled up the makeup bag; it would be going with him in case any last-minute touch-ups were required at the airport. He checked his new watch, a cheap thing from a supermarket; all part of his new look. It was 2:33 A.M.

Once everything was packed away he picked up the carryall with his old suit and old life inside and headed back toward his car. The rest of his escape plan had been carefully scheduled. At 6:30 A.M. he would phone a local taxi company from a call box in the service station, saying that his car had broken down and he was desperate to get to the airport for an 8:30 flight. He had with him not one but two taxi company business cards. Just in case.

Mr. Davies would then be collected and delivered to the airport, where he would check in at the very last minute, so that as little time as possible was spent in the one area from where he could not escape—the departure lounge.

Fincham went back to his car to wait. He sat in silence and his thoughts returned to Marcie Deveraux. Revenge would have been sweet, but escape would be sweeter.

Joey was in a cold, bare cell, waiting for the results of his blood test.

The roadside Breathalyzer had shown him to be way over the legal limit. Joey hadn't needed to wait for the crystals to change color to know that would be the inevitable outcome. He'd been driven to the police station, where two samples of his blood had been taken.

Now all he could do was wait. He'd already been waiting for a long time and he still hadn't smoked his cigar. He was scared; more than that, he was terrified. He'd made a big mistake in drinking as much as he had at the pub. He could take his drink—he felt perfectly sober—but that didn't make any difference. He wasn't the first to make that discovery far too late.

He knew that Elena, Danny and Fergus would be worrying, wondering what had happened, probably thinking that he'd run out on them. But even more than that, he feared what would happen now, once records had been checked and it was discovered that he should have left the country days ago.

It meant either a return to a British prison for a long stretch or the even more terrifying prospect of an escorted flight back to Nigeria.

He sat back on the low bed and heard shouting from another holding cell. Somewhere another drunk was gobbing off about unfair police treatment, demanding to see a solicitor and moaning that the loss of his driving license would ruin him. Joey shook his head; the loss of a driving license was the least of his worries.

Footsteps echoed along the corridor outside the cell. Joey stood up as keys turned in the lock, the door swung open and the police sergeant who had taken down his details earlier appeared in the doorway.

"You must know people in high places, mate."

"I'm sorry?"

"You're leaving us. Lucky boy. Very lucky."

The sergeant stepped to one side and Marcie Deveraux walked into the cell.

43

"I knew he'd do this. I knew he'd let us down in the end."

Elena was furious. After everything that had happened over the last couple of days she had finally begun to believe that perhaps, after all, her dad had changed. But now he'd gone AWOL again. Same old Joey. He would never change. Never.

"I bet he's gone to see that woman! I bet he's . . . I don't want to think about what he's doing. It's disgusting at his age."

"If he's with his girlfriend, at least he's out of trouble for a while," said Danny. "He'll turn up when he's ready."

Elena was standing by the window, staring out into the darkness, vainly hoping to see the rental car pull to a standstill on the road outside the square. But she knew it wouldn't.

Danny wandered over and stood by her side. "Don't worry."

"What makes you think I'm worried?" snapped Elena. "I'm angry, that's all. And pissed off!"

"Yeah, right," said Danny softly.

Fergus was stretched out on the old sofa, thinking about the e-mail he was going to get Elena to send to M. Deveraux.

He had no doubts about the identity of M. Deveraux now. She'd been there all along, manipulating them, waiting until they had outlived their usefulness, planning their elimination.

But they had powerful ammunition of their own now. The information stored on the CDs was their lifeline. The Intelligence and Security Services would never risk that information being revealed to the press. The framing and proposed killing of innocent people would be totally unacceptable to the British people. It was enough to topple the heads of both services *and* bring down the government.

Fergus planned to arrange a meeting with M. Deveraux. He would give her one of the CDs as proof of what they had, along with his demands for the future. As he thought about the e-mail he wanted to send, he was holding the electrician's screwdriver, completing the circuit by placing one thumb on the top contact and touching the end so that the red light in the handle lit up. But as he glanced over at Elena's laptop, he dropped the screwdriver and pulled himself upright. "You'd better come and take a look at this."

The laptop was still online and a pop-up had appeared on screen.

Hey, Elena, How's it going?? Great exploit, eh? Black Star hasn't had so much fun in a long time!!

Danny and Elena stared at the screen.

"He knows your name," said Danny. "How could he do that?"

"We don't even know if Black Star is a *he*," said Elena. "And I've got no idea how he or she knows about me."

She was about to find out.

Surprised I know your real name? Hey, you can't spoof a spoofer!!! Just wanted to say I won't paste your exploit on the

Deep Web, wouldn't want you to get into any trouble!!! Keep in touch, we must work together again. Bye for now.

The screen went blank; Black Star had gone.

Danny looked at Elena. "What was that all about?"

She shrugged. "How should I know? Showing off. Probably spends too much time down in the Deep Web. Should get out more."

Fergus was more concerned with their immediate problems. "I'm ready with that e-mail, Elena. Keep it brief. Just tell her we have everything we need for our continued safety, and we'll be in touch tomorrow to arrange the time and place for a meeting."

Deveraux had changed into operational clothes for the conclusion of her mission, although her working gear carried designer labels. She was wearing Italian blue jeans, a black leather jacket and Nike sneakers.

As they drove away from the police station, Joey kept taking surreptitious sidelong glances as he tried to figure out exactly who his rescuer was and what she wanted.

Deveraux headed away from the main road into the quieter backstreets and for a while she said nothing, deliberately making her nervous passenger wait.

Joey decided he would be the icebreaker. He reached into his jacket pocket for his cigars. "Mind if I smoke? I've been waiting for hours."

"Yes, I do mind," said Deveraux coldly. "You'll have to wait a little longer."

Joey sighed and released his grip on the cigar packet. Once again it was a case of so near, yet so far. Giving up would be easier.

Deveraux took a left turn into a road lined on both sides with parked cars. "So, Joey, where are they?"

"They?" said Joey innocently. "I don't know who you mean."

Deveraux smiled, prepared to play the game for a little while. "Listen, Joey, I'm here to help them, just like I've helped you. Twice now. Getting you out of jail is becoming a habit."

Joey turned and stared at her. "You did that? Before?"

She nodded. "Of course. And that's how I learned about tonight's little escapade. You're on our system, Joey. As soon as your name was fed into the police computer it came through to my people. You should have left the country, as you were told to."

"Yeah, look, I'm sorry, I—"

Deveraux took her left hand from the steering wheel and placed it reassuringly on Joey's arm. "Never mind. You made a mistake. I can sort it out. I can arrange for you to stay here, even get you a UK passport."

"You can?"

"It's just a question of mutual cooperation. You help me and I'll help you."

Joey was thinking quickly: maybe this might yet turn out a lot better than he had feared. "I'd like to help, but I wouldn't want to cause problems for anyone else."

Deveraux took a right; the road was quieter, less built up. "There's no fear of that, Joey. I already know that Fergus is totally innocent. The person I want is about to be taken. All that's needed now is for me to talk to Fergus and the two kids and then everyone can get on with their lives. And that includes you."

She spoke softly and calmly. She seemed so sincere. And so friendly. Genuinely concerned for their welfare.

Joey glanced at her again. She was an attractive woman; beautiful in a cold and detached way. He decided it was time to turn on his famous charm. "I don't even know your name, and when I'm talking to a beautiful woman, I like to know her name."

Deveraux smiled. There was no harm in him knowing. Not now. "It's Marcie."

"Marcie. That's a lovely name. Are you married, Marcie?"

Deveraux laughed, she couldn't stop herself. This sad, deluded individual was actually attempting to chat her up. "No, Joey, I'm not married. Too busy sorting out other people's problems."

"But you do get time off?"

"Business before pleasure, Joey, that's my rule."

It had gone on for long enough. It was time to get this over with and move on. "Now, let's cut the crap, shall we?" She held up a bunch of keys. "The car you were driving was hired on Elena's bank card. I've checked. As well as the car key, there are the keys to an industrial unit on this keyring. And they have an address tag. Careless, Joey. Very careless. That's where they are, isn't it? That's where they're hiding."

Joey didn't reply. And Deveraux didn't need an answer; she had it all figured out. She knew precisely where Fergus, Danny and Elena were hiding.

There was a soft ping on her Xda. She slowed the car and lifted the Xda up to read the brief e-mail Elena had sent. She smiled. "Is that so?" she said softly.

"Problem?" said Joey.

"No problem at all. Everything is fine, but I need to respond to this e-mail."

Up ahead was a deserted stretch of wasteland close to some buildings ready for demolition. It was exactly what Deveraux had been looking for. She pulled the vehicle off the road, drove slowly into a dark, unlit area and switched off the engine. "You get out and have your cigar—you've waited long enough."

Joey needed no second invitation. He pushed open the door, pulled his cigars and lighter from his pocket and took a few steps away from the vehicle. Deveraux saw the blue smoke curl into the night air. The condemned man was enjoying his last smoke.

Deveraux had already decided on the method. Going to the ready bag for a weapon and loading up was not the right option. Joey was stupid, but not that stupid. He would try to run, and that would mean an unnecessary delay and complications. There was a much simpler way, once Joey had had a few more puffs of his last cigar.

Deveraux flicked the car's internal light switch to off so that her victim would get no warning as she opened her door. Noiselessly she stepped from the vehicle. Joey didn't hear a thing as she approached, silent as a panther.

With a few light steps she was behind him. She held her Xda in her right hand, swung it around hard and fast and heard it connect with Joey's nose. There was a dull crunch of fracturing bone as the big man fell to his knees, holding his face as blood poured between his fingers.

Deveraux dropped to her knees behind him, stuck the phone's edge across his throat with her right hand and gripped the other side with her left. She pulled back on the Xda. Joey was kicking out, arms flailing as he tried to tear the phone away from his neck, but Deveraux responded by leaning forward, using the weight of her upper body to bend Joey's head down so that his chin was virtually touching his chest. She wrenched the phone back even harder.

Joey's legs kicked out again; his body jerked as he frantically tried to free himself. He couldn't breathe, his head was dizzy, his vision blurred. His hands scrabbled at Deveraux's face, but he was weakening quickly, and his assassin simply moved her head to avoid his desperate hands.

It took another minute, no more. Then Joey's movements subsided to a little spasmodic twitching of the legs. And then there was no movement at all.

Deveraux let go of the phone with one hand and Joey's limp body slumped to the ground. She checked for a pulse in his neck; there was nothing.

Joey's last cigar was still smoldering on the ground, close to his body. As Deveraux started to turn away, one foot made contact with a small cardboard packet lying in the dirt. She smiled. "Should have read what it says on the packet, Joey. Smoking kills."

"Ray . . . Ray . . . There's a few Rays, but no Sonny."

"This is pointless," said Danny as he watched Elena working at her laptop. "You haven't got an address and you don't even know if Sonny is his real name. It's probably not; it's probably just a nickname. You know, sun ray, Sonny Ray. His real name could be anything."

Elena sighed with irritation. "I'm not stupid, Danny. Course I know that. But Sonny is all we've got."

That much was true. They knew Joey's former business partner went by the name of Sonny Ray—it said precisely that on the sign above the unit. And Sonny was married to Joyce, so Elena was doing all she could do to trace Joyce. If she found Joyce, she would find Joey. That was the theory, anyway.

The long night was passing slowly. Danny and Elena were both tired, and touchy, and worried. Whatever Joey had been up to, he should have returned hours ago, or at least called. He had Elena's mobile number and had been instructed to use no names if he did get in touch. But Joey just didn't seem capable of following instructions.

Elena had tried online phone listings and the Yellow Pages, searching for either a Sonny or a Joyce Ray. It was proving to be a fruitless exploit.

"He could have had an accident in the car," said Danny. "Might be sitting in a police station now."

"Or a hospital," said Elena.

Fergus had been listening to their bickering for too long. "Look, you two, give it a rest. Wherever he is, we have to assume that our situation here might be compromised. If he doesn't show up by an hour and a half before first light then we have to get out."

"But how can you," asked Danny, "without Joey to drive us?"

"I'll manage," said his grandfather firmly. All three of them looked at Fergus's leg. The dressing was leaking blood and pus, and at that moment it didn't look as though he could even stand, let alone manage.

"And then what?"

"We stick to the plan. I meet up with our friend; give her one of the disks to prove that we know all about the whole operation. She's in for a bit of a surprise when she hears the deal I'm going to offer her. I want new identities for us all, and Fincham out of the way, like she said. If anything happens to us, at any time, the press gets the document. While she chews that one over, we'll lie low and wait."

Danny had listened closely to everything his grandfather said, but Elena's thoughts were still with Joey. She powered down her laptop and slammed down the top far harder than she would nor-mally have done. "If he is in hospital, it's his own stupid fault," she almost shouted. "He's stupid. Stupid!"

Danny was about to say that he knew Elena didn't mean what she'd said. But he saw the tears in her eyes. He kept his mouth shut. Elena was hurting.

Fergus knew it too. "We should grab a little sleep while we can. You two get your heads down, I'll take first stag."

"No, I will," said Elena. "I won't sleep anyway."

Outside, Marcie Deveraux had paused by the metal shutters just as she heard Elena's raised voice. They were in there. No doubt now.

Deveraux had left her car outside the square, and out of sight of the window. She was totally confident of her own supreme skill and ability in action. Few people were her equal. Watts was, she knew that. He could not be underestimated, so her approach to the unit had been slow and ultracautious.

She kept to the shadows, hugged the walls and moved silently and cautiously. Now that she had all the confirmation required, she used exactly the same method to return to her car. She reached the vehicle and dialed a number on her Xda.

George Fincham was sitting in his car, calmly drinking disgusting service station tea from a Styrofoam cup when his official secure mobile began to ring. He had planned that it would be one of the last things he would dispose of, just in case an official call came through. Even so, he was surprised to hear it ring at this hour of the morning.

He looked at the screen and saw Deveraux's name appear. He

felt his anger begin to rise; only the name Fergus Watts could cause equal fury within him now.

But he sounded calm and assured as he pressed the answer button and spoke softly. "Yes, Marcie?"

Deveraux sounded equally calm. "I'm sorry to call at this hour, sir. But it's important."

"Go on."

"Watts, sir. I know where he is. With the boy and an unknown female around Danny's age."

"I see. And your plan is?"

"We could finish this together, sir, before first light. There isn't time to gather the team, and if we leave it they may move and we could lose them again. It could all be over within an hour, sir."

Fincham hesitated, his mind racing. "Do you have a ready bag? I shall need a weapon."

"I have everything we need, sir."

Fincham began pulling off the false beard he was wearing. An hour. It still gave him time, plenty of time. He picked up the pen and one of the taxi company business cards and turned it over. "Very well, Marcie, give me an RV. We'll do it, we'll clear everything up tonight."

They decided on the RV and hung up. Deveraux smiled. *Clear everything up,* Fincham had said. That was exactly what she had begun to do. She had already called in the Firm's "cleaners" to arrange for Joey's body to be collected and disposed of; it would be done by now.

There was one further call to make while she waited for Fincham's arrival. Dudley might not be happy about being woken at this hour of the morning, but he had insisted on being kept fully informed of all developments, at whatever hour.

But Dudley wasn't sleeping: he instantly answered Deveraux's call to his secure phone. "Be quick, Marcie, and I may have to cut you off—I'm waiting for a call of my own."

Deveraux was slightly taken aback, but she made her report quickly. "First part of the operation completed, sir. Everything else will be within the hour."

"Good. Report to me then."

The line went dead and Deveraux looked at her Xda, puzzled. She had expected more than that; a "Well done" or even a few questions. Dudley's own call must be important.

It was. Dudley was in his office, and his thoughts were focused on a different operation. He'd been waiting for the crucial information he'd been promised. When it came through he immediately called the Prime Minister's private secretary, who knew better than to argue about the PM being disturbed at this hour. He simply asked Dudley to hold while he woke his boss.

The Prime Minister came on the line. "Yes, Dudley?"

Dudley wasted no time. "The bombings, Prime Minister. We have a lead at last. A significant lead."

44

It was like a deadly game of cat and mouse, and both Deveraux and Fincham believed that *they* were the cat.

The MP5 SD was resting across Deveraux's lap as she put her foot down hard on the accelerator pedal. Fincham was in the passenger seat, the Sig 9 mm pistol from Deveraux's ready bag in his right hand and the keys to the unit in his left.

They had met and swiftly prepared for the attack in a pitch-dark parking space behind the Renault showroom, less than a minute away from the unit. Deveraux quickly went through the details and Fincham listened in silence, nodding that he understood exactly what his role would be.

He was backup, which was the correct procedure. Deveraux was the skilled and highly trained operative; she was used to killing. Fincham had been deskbound for years and he knew that if he insisted on leading the attack it would arouse his second in command's suspicions.

So he listened and made ready the Sig as Deveraux told him the plan. She would go up the stairs first. The suppressed MP5 would allow her to kill Watts and the two teenagers in virtual silence, so as not to alert any all-night workers in the nearby Parcel Force depot. The last thing they needed was the police turning up in response to an emergency call.

Fincham was only to use the pistol if Deveraux got into trouble. They couldn't be certain that Watts was unarmed, and although Deveraux was good, like all good operators she knew her limitations.

Fincham had insisted on only one thing: the attack had to be hard and fast. He was the boss, and this time Deveraux made no complaint. She had planned another covert approach to get inside the unit unheard, but she quickly reasoned that a speedy shock hit might even be preferable. Fincham didn't have her skills; with a covert approach he could give them away. So hard and fast it would be. It didn't matter to Deveraux; the results would be the same: they were all going to die.

As they neared the service road, her boss was thinking exactly the same thing: they were all going to die. Once Deveraux had taken care of Watts and the kids, it would be her turn—a double tap to the head. If any nearby workers were alerted by the two shots then so be it. He would be away in seconds, heading for Heathrow and that eight-thirty flight to Moscow. There would be just time to change back into his disguise and redo his false beard and makeup.

They reached the service road and Deveraux glanced at her boss. "Are you ready, sir?"

"Oh, yes, Marcie. Quite ready."

Deveraux hit the gas and the engine screamed at full revs as they headed for the entrance to the square.

She dropped to second gear as she took the right turn. Her foot was still hard down as they hurtled toward the unit, which was to their right. Her left hand gripped the hand brake. She calmly gave

Fincham the warning, "Stand by," and he opened his door and held it open.

Deveraux yanked the wheel in a complete circle to the right, pulled up on the hand brake, took her foot off the gas and hit the brakes. The car spun around as the hand brake turn pointed the car back toward the entrance.

Fincham jumped out and ran toward the unit's shutter door. Deveraux leaped from the vehicle and ran around the front, pulling out her SD's collapsible stock and putting it to her shoulder as Fincham pushed open the door.

Both eyes open, safety catch off, trigger finger taking the slack first pressure so that she could fire more quickly, Deveraux ran into the building.

The surprise attack was working. Elena had been on stag. Despite her protests that she wouldn't sleep, she was desperately tired after the efforts and stress of the night, and soon after the others drifted off she too was dozing.

She woke as the car screeched to a halt. She was certain Joey had returned; probably in trouble as usual, but at least he was back. She jumped up and ran to the window as Fergus and Danny stirred. But it was already too late. Their attackers were in the building.

"It's not my dad!" screamed Elena. "It's not him!"

Deveraux was at the foot of the stairs, weapon pointing up at the floor above. Fincham was close behind, and as she got her first sight of the upper level, the spill from the external security lighting revealed exactly what she was hoping to see. "Stand still! Don't move!"

Fergus had pulled himself to his feet and was standing by the sofa and one of the old freezers they had carried upstairs for protection from the PAD. His arms were outstretched to show that he was no threat. Deveraux quickly spotted the bloodstained leg and then her eyes flicked to Danny and Elena standing by the wall to her right. She moved up into the room. "Against the walls! Move! Sit down against the walls!"

Danny and Elena slid quickly down the wall as Fergus took two hobbling backward steps and painfully lowered himself to the ground. He was sitting on something, and as Deveraux turned momentarily to see Fincham warily appear at the top of the stairs, Fergus reached down and his hand closed around the electrician's screwdriver. It had fallen to the floor as he stood up.

"Get on with it, Marcie!" shouted Fincham. "Kill them! Kill them!" He glared at Fergus. "Kill them!"

Fincham could wait no longer; he began to raise his pistol. But then Deveraux quickly spun back to him with her weapon still at her shoulder. "Change of plan. You first—*you* have a weapon."

Fincham's face registered one moment of horror and disbelief; there was no time for anything else. Deveraux squeezed second pressure and the dull thuds of a double tap sounded as Fincham was hit in the body and sent crashing down the stairs.

The assassin swiveled her weapon back to Fergus. "Now you."

"Wait!" shouted Fergus. "We have the Secret Ultra document! We know your real plan! We have Secret Ultra!"

Deveraux released first pressure. "Impossible!"

"It's not impossible, we've got it!"

She hesitated, trying to work out the implications of what Fergus was saying. It was a bluff; it had to be a bluff.

"The document you wrote about Fincham and me, Marcie, I saw your signature. And we've burned CDs of it! And they're safe!"

The CDs were far from safe. They were in Fergus's pocket; he was just trying to buy time.

As the seconds passed, Danny saw a tiny red flashing light coming from his grandfather's left hand. It was close to the floor, unseen by Deveraux, who was standing to Fergus's right. It was a message; Danny knew his grandfather was sending him a message. He concentrated hard as the light continued to flash and Fergus attempted to bargain for their lives.

"They're in a safe place. If I don't report in tomorrow, they go to the press. You, *Marcie,* exposed as a murderer."

He kept on completing the circuit on the screwdriver, praying that Danny would understand what the flashes meant.

-.-.   ---   ...-   .   .-.

As soon as Deveraux had ordered Fergus to sit by the wall, he had made his decision. He was less than a meter from the power socket and plug for the PAD. He was going to try to detonate the device, but he had to get Danny and Elena to move first. If they could reach the protection of the sofa and the two freezers in front of it, they might survive the fearsome explosion.

He too would have a chance of survival: the old cooker and another freezer were between him and the back of the PAD. But he didn't care about himself now. He'd been close to death many times. It could have happened in Northern Ireland, or Colombia, or five or six other places. If it were to happen now, then so be it. All that mattered was that he saved Danny and Elena.

"Are you really gonna take the chance that I'm bluffing, Marcie? *Are* you?"

Deveraux had thought it through. Watts *was* bluffing: he could not have accessed the secret file, even if he knew of the existence of SECRET: ULTRA itself. "Good try, Watts, but a lot of effort for one more minute of life."

She took first pressure, but before she could fire the shutter downstairs rattled. She heard footsteps. Fincham—he was trying to escape. "Shit!"

Deveraux moved back to the stairs and ran down to the bottom. She heard the vehicle start up. A problem, but she would get Fincham later. It was time to finish Watts and the kids. The car's engine roared and the tires screeched.

Fergus knew that this was his moment. He screamed one word: "Now!" and dived for the plug. As he pushed it into the socket, Danny grabbed Elena, pulled her to the sofa and threw himself over her body.

There was no time to look back. Fergus turned on the power and the world became a blinding flash of white.

EPILOGUE

They were in a room with high frosted glass windows. Wire ran through the toughened glass. They had no idea where they were, although the occasional sound of jet engines suggested a military base of some description.

Neither of them remembered much about the explosion. The flash of brilliant light, a shock wave of incredible heat, the first thump of deafening noise. And then nothing. Not even the pain. The pain had come later, after they had woken up.

Elena was the first. Danny had saved her from the very worst of the explosion. The freezers had crashed into the sofa, which had been shredded by the vicious salvo of shattered glass and brickwork. But the foam padding protected them, as the sofa and they were hurled across the room.

Mercifully they had passed out, and as Elena drifted back to consciousness, she thought the urgent voices she heard were a dream. Then she thought her dad was calling to her. In pitch darkness she heard herself weakly muttering, "Dad . . . Dad . . . Da—"

And then she passed out again. It may have been for seconds, or minutes. She didn't know. When she came around for a second time, the crushing weight on top of her had been shifted and a medic was staring down at her. Elena just saw the smile.

"Dad?" she whispered again.

"I'm not your dad," said the smiling medic. "But I'm glad you're awake."

As her eyes slowly cleared, she turned her head and saw Danny lying next to her among the rubble. Two more medics were trying to bring him around.

Across the devastated room a limp body was being maneuvered down what remained of the mangled stairs. And then Elena realized. It was Fergus. They were carrying Fergus's body down the stairs.

After that everything happened quickly. Elena and Danny were carried out on stretchers to a darkened ambulance and driven away swiftly. They seemed to be on the road for hours and both received medical attention as the vehicle was moving.

Elena was cut and bruised, every part of her body seemed tender. Her hair and eyebrows were singed and there was a painful flash burn to one arm. Her hearing had suffered the most. Her ears were ringing and although she could just hear words directed at her, they were muffled, almost as though she were underwater.

Danny had fared worse. There were more cuts, and deeper bruises, and his hearing was in the same underwaterlike state. But more worrying was the acute pain in his side. He was finding it difficult to even breathe.

The ambulance had drawn to a halt and the rear doors were opened directly onto a corridor with no windows. It was no ordinary hospital; it felt like a prison. Danny was rushed away on his stretcher for X-rays, while Elena was taken to the room where they both were now.

A nurse, who said nothing while she worked, treated Elena's cuts and the burn. And then a white-coated doctor came in and gave her a more thorough check. He looked into her eyes and her ears, and when he said he thought there would be no permanent damage, Elena realized that her hearing was slowly returning to normal.

She was left alone; confused, disoriented and afraid. She was convinced now that she was in some sort of prison and that they had only patched up her wounds in preparation for the interrogation that was to follow.

On the other side of the locked door, Elena heard a guard shuffling about in the corridor and the fear increased.

Fergus was dead, her dad had disappeared again; there was only Danny now. She wanted him there with her.

Some time later—Elena couldn't tell how long—the door was unlocked and opened.

A guard stood in the doorway, wearing a pistol on a belt holster. He stared at Elena and then stepped back. Danny was in a wheelchair being pushed by a nurse.

Once Danny was in the room, the nurse left without a word and the guard pulled the door shut and relocked it.

Danny's head was bandaged and there was a dressing, identical to that on Elena's arm, on one of his hands.

They sat side by side in a still-stunned silence for a while, and then Danny said suddenly, "Fractured ribs. Doctor said they should mend quickly."

Elena nodded, waiting for the question she was dreading.

"But they won't tell me anything about my granddad. Do you know what happened to him?"

Elena did know, of course she knew, but she couldn't say it. Not then. But she didn't want to lie to Danny. "No one's told me anything."

She looked away, pretending to examine the hardened, protective plastic coating that had been sprayed on the burns on her arm. "Maybe they'll tell us. Soon." She wanted to change the subject. "How did you know what to do?"

"My granddad; he was signaling 'Cover' in Morse code. I knew he meant us to get behind the sofa."

They fell back into silence, both of them reliving the horrific moments leading up to the explosion.

There were footsteps in the corridor and the door was unlocked. Marcie Deveraux entered the room, with the guard following. She was wearing a neck brace and walked stiffly. At the moment of the explosion she had been flung back against the wall at the bottom of the stairs. Her black hair was singed and her eyebrows had disappeared. There were cuts around her eyes and her bottom lip was swollen.

"It's over," she said when she saw the fear in Danny and Elena's eyes. "You have no need to be afraid."

"My granddad?" said Danny quickly. "Where is he?"

Deveraux paused for a moment. "Here."

"Is he . . . ? Is he all right?"

"You'll see him soon."

Elena knew the answer to the question Deveraux had neatly avoided, but all she could do was wait until Danny learned the truth and then be there to help him. But she had a question of her own. "My dad? Have you found him?"

Deveraux replied without a flicker of emotion, "Probably lying low somewhere." She went to Danny's wheelchair, eased off the brake and then looked at Elena. "We have questions for you both. Can you walk? I can send for another wheelchair."

"I don't need your help," said Elena, struggling to her feet. "I'll walk."

Deveraux shrugged and pushed Danny to the door. A jet aircraft engine screamed overhead, and as they moved down a long corridor with no windows and only fluorescent lighting overhead, the guard followed behind them.

The building seemed to be laid out in a square. At the end of the corridor they turned to the left and continued until they came to a closed office door, where Deveraux knocked once. She turned to the guard. "That will be all. Thank you."

The guard nodded, and as Deveraux opened the door, he turned and walked away.

They could see inside the surprisingly large room. To the right a man was sitting behind a desk, and on top of the desk was Elena's battered laptop. It was open.

The man smiled. "Come in, please."

Deveraux nodded for Elena to go into the room and she walked through, her eyes fixed on the laptop.

"I'm afraid we're going to have to provide you with a new one," said the man. "My name is Dudley. I hope we are going to be friends."

"Friends!" said Danny angrily as Deveraux wheeled him through the doorway. "After what you've done to us? And my granddad!"

"Yes," said Dudley with a sigh. "It has all been rather . . . unfortunate. But—"

"I want to see him! Where is he!"

"I'm here, Danny," said a voice from behind them.

Danny looked back. The far end of the room had been hidden

from view as they passed through the open door. Fergus was lying, half raised up, in a hospital bed.

"Granddad!" said Danny, pushing himself up from the wheel-chair. He'd never called him Granddad before—not to his face; he'd never been able to do that. But now the word burst out at the joy of seeing Fergus alive.

He was alive. In a mess, but alive. His head was bandaged; so were both his hands, and next to the hospital bed there was a stand with blood and plasma bottles. Tubes ran into Fergus's left arm.

Danny struggled to operate the wheelchair and Elena grabbed the handles and pushed it across the room so that he could sit at the bedside. "I thought . . . I thought . . ."

"Yeah, me too," said Fergus weakly. "The cooker saved me—they built those old ones to last."

"What about Fincham?" said Danny. "Did he get away?"

Dudley got up from his chair and moved around the desk. "George Fincham is dead. Your grandfather's explosive device was extremely effective." He glanced at the assorted cuts and bruises on all their faces. "Perhaps a little too effective. But the whole matter is now satisfactorily concluded. The Secret Ultra file was erased, and as far as we are concerned it never existed."

"What about the other ones who've been after us for the past six months? What happens to them?"

"Fran and her team were completely unaware that they were operating illegally for Fincham. Their future is secure."

"So that's it?" said Danny. "Can we just go? Are we free?"

Dudley paused for a moment. "Your grandfather and I have been having a long conversation about that."

Danny and Elena looked at Fergus, and he nodded at them reassuringly before Dudley continued.

"You see, we need your help."

"Our help?" said Elena.

"You've shown remarkable skill and ingenuity over the past few months. We would like you to work for us, on a temporary basis to begin with, and on a very specific operation." He glanced across the room. "With Miss Deveraux."

Danny stared at his grandfather. "Is this for real? She wanted to kill us—all of us."

Deveraux didn't appear any happier about the prospect of teaming up with her former adversaries than they were. But she was a professional. "That was in a previous mission. That mission is now concluded satisfactorily."

"And it's as easy as that for you, is it?"

Deveraux's face gave away nothing.

Fergus shifted slightly in the bed. "Just listen to what Dudley has to say, then I'll have my say."

Dudley nodded his thanks to him. "The teenage suicide bombings—I'm sure you've heard about them."

"Yeah, we've heard."

"We want you to help us catch the person orchestrating these attacks," said Deveraux.

"But why us? What can we do?"

Dudley walked back to his desk and sat on the corner, with his hand resting on Elena's laptop. "You see, all three of the unfortunate young men were recruited through the Internet, and as we now know, Miss Omolodon is quite an expert on the Internet."

"There are plenty of experts out there," said Elena. "And I prefer to be called by my first name."

Dudley smiled. "Before each bombing, the young men tore out the hard drives of their own computers and destroyed them. But our own experts have managed to find a link between them by studying the screen burns on the computers themselves. All this modern technology is beyond me, but I'm sure you understand, Miss Om— Elena."

"Yeah, but I still don't see why you need us."

"Not only me. The Prime Minister himself has requested that you help us in this mission."

Danny laughed. "Yeah, right. The Prime Minister needs *our* help?"

But Dudley wasn't laughing. "The whole nation needs your help, Danny."

"They're asking a lot of you, Danny," said Fergus. "To my mind, too much. But I can't tell you what to do: I've run your life and made your decisions for long enough. It's up to you now. Both of you." He looked at Dudley. "Tell them about the screen burns."

"Yes, of course. The screen burns revealed exactly why we need you to help us in this crisis. Just two words."

Danny looked at Elena and then back at Dudley. "What were they?"

"Black Star."

THE END

Morse Code Alphabet

A .−	N −.	0 −−−−−
B −...	O −−−	1 .−−−−
C −.−.	P .−−.	2 ..−−−
D −..	Q −−.−	3 ...−−
E .	R .−.	4 ....−
F ..−.	S ...	5 .....
G −−.	T −	6 −....
H	U ..−	7 −−...
I ..	V ...−	8 −−−..
J .−−−	W .−−	9 −−−−.
K −.−	X −..−	Fullstop .−.−.−
L .−..	Y −.−−	Comma −−..−−
M −−	Z −−..	Query ..−−..